Late

Summer Love

By

AWARD-WINNING & NATIONAL BESTSELLING AUTHOR
PAT SIMMONS

Cover and interior: Fiverr
Copy editor: Chandra Sparks Splond
Proofreader: Judicious Revisions LLC,
Fiverr/Creative01
Beta readers: Stacey Jefferson, Darlene Simmons, and Shannan Harper

ISBN-13: 978-1546583189
ISBN-10: 1546583181

Acknowledgments

Special thanks to Deandre Bell, Troop-E 1st- 230th AHB (Assault Helicopter Battalion), for inspiring *Late Summer Love*.

Then enters Detective Michael Moore Sr., St. Louis County Police, for filling in the blanks. Thanks to Jim Powell and his wife, Kim, for helping it all make sense.

Shout out to my cousin, Adriene Langford-Harris, Veterans Administration, Indianapolis, for bringing me full circle. I couldn't have finished this story without your help.

To all the men and women who serve our country, thank you.

For the many, many readers from military bases from March Air Reserve Base, Riverside County, California, to Patrick AFB, Brevard County, Florida, and many in between, especially Scott AFB, Illinois, where Dave, Allen, Joyce Renee and so many others have supported my book signings and read my stories over the past ten years. *Late Summer Love* is dedicated to you!

In memory of my nephew, Private Heary Joe

Eastern Jr., U.S. Army
1981–2000
Gone too soon, but never forgotten

Chapter 1

First week in August…

"You may now salute your bride," Minister Ray announced, grinning at the newlyweds.

The moment was surreal as the first tear trickled down Paige Blake's cheek, then a second. Sucking in her breath, she waited for their lips to touch and seal their commitment. Her vision blurred as she closed her eyes, then a thunderous applause snapped her back into reality. It wasn't her wedding. She was only the maid of honor. Sniffing, Paige wiped at her tears and remembered to clap.

Her best friend and confidant, Dominique Hayes, was officially Mrs. Ashton Taylor. Paige exhaled. It was going to be a big adjustment not to be able to pick up the phone and chat first thing in the mornings or late into the night. Forget about weekend get-togethers.

Their friendship had begun in high school and had survived and thrived into their thirties. They had shared woes, victories, secrets, and more. Now, Paige would be solo, waving the white flag of singlehood on the sidelines.

She wasn't desperate, but at thirty-three—soon to be thirty-four—where was that godly man with a one-of-a kind love for her? Before she knew it, she would be in her mid-thirties, then forties. Maybe by the time she received her

AARP card, there would be someone in her life to at least hold her hand.

Paige was depressing herself, and this really was a happy occasion, but—and there always was a "but"—maybe God had forgotten about her.

If God sent a practicing Christian man to her front door, literally, as He had done for Dominique, Paige wouldn't let him knock twice. Ashton was a courier for a logistics company and happened to deliver a package to Dominique's doorstep. As of today, the rest was history.

The moment was bittersweet. Isn't this what she and Dominique had waited, prayed, and believed God for—a mate?

Clearing her throat, Paige fell into step behind the bride and groom with her handsome groomsman, who was also happily married and the father of two. Didn't Ashton have any single friends or family members?

Rejoice with those who rejoice, weep with those who weep. God whispered Romans 12:15 as guests continued to applaud until they left the sanctuary.

Ashamed from the Lord's rebuke, Paige repented, then submitted to the Holy Ghost, so envy or jealousy wouldn't rise up within her. Her soul cried out, *God, help me. I'm trying, but I'm hurting.* When she eyed a photographer pointing the camera her way, she put on a winning smile.

Paige couldn't love Dominique more than a sister. Both wanted summer weddings, and Dominique's color scheme was stunning: sage dresses for the four bridesmaids and gray tuxes and sage bow ties for the men. It was truly a stunning combination.

As the wedding party formed the receiving line in the adjacent reception hall, Paige stepped out of position to hug her dear friend. "I'm happy for you," she choked out.

Dominique pulled her back and looked into her eyes. "Your time is coming soon—maybe today," she said, a hopeful gleam in her eye as happiness glowed from Dominique and Ashton's faces.

"Places please," the organizer instructed. Glancing around, Paige was the only one out of place, so she dutifully returned to her post.

Paige and Dominique had been inseparable, attending their church's singles ministry meetings, as well as hanging out on the weekends and during summer traveling explorations. The newlyweds were honeymooning in Madrid, Spain of all places. She and Dominique were planning that trip once Paige had landed another job after being laid off. She just needed to earn vacation time and save more money. While Dominique waited, Ashton stepped in.

Paige's summer vacation would be a road trip in a week to Charleston for the Blake and Croft family reunion. Originally, her aunts in Phoenix were hosting it, but at the last minute, her South Carolina family took over. At least, she would be on the beach.

The stream of well-wishers shook hands with the bridal party as they made their way to Dominique and Ashton. A few who knew Paige whispered, "You're next," and added a hopeful smile.

Paige nodded politely and hoped that God had given them that prophecy. Otherwise, she was thankful for the encouragement.

By the time the bridal party was seated at the head table, Paige had identified some potential prospects. If they were single, she needed proof that their salvation walk with the

Lord was strong. Until then, she was determined to guard her heart, which was crying out to God to remember her.

When it was time for the toasts, Paige listened to all the blessings and happy wishes given to the bride and groom. When it was her turn, she stood and lifted her champagne glass of sparkling white grape juice. "To my best friend…sister…and now the one and only Mrs. Ashton Taylor—" she added humor to mask her emotions, then swallowed—"I'm so happy that God has blessed you. You and Ashton are a perfect match. My prayer for you is happiness, long life, and a double set of twins." As the audience laughed, she and Dominique shared a knowing smile. Her friend wanted four children. Dominique blew her a kiss. The gesture warmed her heart, and they both mouthed, *I love you.*

When Mr. and Mrs. Taylor graced the floor for their first dance, it took Paige's breath away. She knew how much Dominique loved her new husband—she heard about it for months. But the look of love in Ashton's eyes for his bride triggered every romantic fairytale cartoon, movie, and book Paige had stored in her mind. The awe on Ashton's face made her want to binge on a romantic comedy marathon for a week.

It wasn't long before the organizer stood behind the mic stand. "Calling all the single ladies. Please take center stage."

With her bouquet in hand, Dominique glided past Paige. "You better catch this," she mumbled." Dominique made eye contact with Paige and frowned. Clearly, Paige wasn't in the right position. Not quite discreetly, she tilted her head and gritted her teeth to the place where she wanted Paige, as if Dominique was setting up a formation with team players to make a basket. Paige complied.

Within seconds, the bouquet toss was high like a fly baseball to the outfield. Ladies moved as if it was a coordinated dance step, hoping for the bouquet to land in their hands. It was within Paige's reach, then in the blink of an eye, she was robbed when bridesmaid Dedra King bumped her out of the way and snatched the bouquet.

As everyone cheered, Paige's heart dropped. Another missed opportunity.

Chapter 2

Second week in August...

Blake Cross was no longer on a mission. With his DD214 papers of military separation, he was back on U.S. soil in Cleveland, Ohio, permanently. After three tours of active duty in Iraq and Afghanistan, plus two years with the Ohio National Guard, the military had been in his DNA for fourteen years.

He had been a civilian for six weeks. How long would it take for him to readjust to a life where he didn't have to answer to anyone?

One day you will answer to Me.

God? What did I do? What do You mean? When no answer came, Blake decided to brush it off to his imagination. Besides, he was in Charleston, South Carolina, for the weekend. Grabbing his key card, Blake strolled out of his hotel room in search of family to reconnect with after his long absence.

Leave it to the Bells and Crosses to choose another historic site for their family reunion. The DoubleTree Hotel was spacious for his hundred-plus family members to gather. After decades of hosting family reunions, there was no shortage of African-American historically significant places for organizers to designate as this year's must-see spot. He wouldn't be surprised one day if everybody ended up in Africa where Ancestry.com had pinpointed their descendants.

Walking out of his third-floor suite, he admired the hotel's stately layout leading to the elevator. Once there, he pushed the down button and waited. When the doors opened, a sweet fragrance beckoned him to come in. He did, and his knees weakened. It took all his willpower not to drool. *Wow*. He was in the company of the most exotic woman he had seen in a long, long time.

How could a woman have so much hair? Shiny black curls glistened. It reminded him of the dolls his older sisters had when he was a boy. However, this woman wasn't a toy. Her delicate fragrance filled the elevator like a garden, but it wasn't overpowering. She removed fashionable shades from her face, and hypnotic hazel eyes stared back at him. That was it. He stopped breathing. Call for resuscitation now!

"Hi. Here for the reunion?" she asked, snapping him out of the trance.

Getting his bearings, Blake took short breaths and recovered. "Yep. It's been a long time since I've attended one."

She nodded as the doors closed without him selecting his stop. "I didn't think you looked familiar. I'm Paige Blake from St. Louis, Miranda and William's daughter." She extended her hand, and the softness seemed to melt in his. When his heart skipped a beat, he released it immediately. He had chased after many women in his days, but none that were in his bloodline.

Whoever Aunt or Cousin Miranda was, she has a pretty daughter, definitely a looker. She probably had men

11

straining their necks to appreciate her beauty. Come to think of it, the Crosses were known for having nice-looking children. His older sisters were evidence of that. Monique and Sanette had their pick of men until they decided which ones couldn't get away. He had yet to meet a woman who would fit that description. "I'm Blake from Cleveland, Lily and—"

The doors opened to the lower level and they walked out in sync, without him finishing.

"I know that, silly. This *is* the Blake/Croft reunion. Do you know where our hospitality suite is?" She squinted, and they pointed at the same time in opposite directions.

Blake saw it first. "There it is…Cross/Bell Reunion, the Queen Bee Room."

"The Majesty Room…" she said at the same time. Paige frowned. "Cross/Bell? Aren't you with the Blake/Croft reunion?" Her bewildered expression begged for an explanation. "I assumed you were saying you're a Blake versus a Croft cousin."

"It appears our family reunions are sharing this hotel this weekend." Blake snickered with renewed interest, relieved there was a mix-up.

"Paige," a woman's squeal echoed from the far end of the hall. "You finally made it!"

Twirling around, Paige released her own high-pitched squeal. The two started a trek toward each other. Without a goodbye, he had been dismissed, leaving a dusting of intrigue behind. Despite separate family reunions, he planned to reunite with Paige before the weekend ended.

"Who was that?" Nyla Blake, her cousin and her roommate for the weekend, demanded once they were behind closed doors of the hospitality suite. Her hazel eyes—a Blake trademark—sparkled with mischief. Both were the same height—about five-six—and the same shade of golden brown. Another trademark was a head full of thick hair, if they didn't cut it. Nyla did, and the short cut enhanced her looks.

"His name is Blake. We rode down the elevator together." Paige shrugged as she surveyed the stuff to be handed out tonight during the Friday night reunion kickoff banquet.

Her cousin's shoulders slumped. "Should have known. Are we related to all the fine men?"

"I hope not," Paige said nonchalantly as she peeped at the prizes, awards, and other recognitions that were stacked in categories, but there were still more piles that needed separating. "That's his first name." She paused and twisted her lips. "I can't recall if he told me his last name or not, but he's here for another reunion. Strange, huh?" She couldn't recall two family reunions occupying the same hotel at the same time in all her years attending.

"Excellent." Nyla grinned. "Can't do the kissing cousins thing. Maybe I'll push all the floors next time so I can catch a ride on the elevator with him."

Shaking her head, Paige chuckled at her cousin's plotting. Single, too, Nyla was two years older and more aggressive on the dating scene. She had no preferences on nationality—Paige didn't either—but Nyla had stipulations like he had to have money to pamper her every whim. Paige wanted a mate whose mission was to walk with God. A godly husband meant a godly home, and that's what she wanted.

"Go for it, cuz." Paige was still emotionally drained after Dominique's wedding. She saw pure love in action, and it was a tough act to follow without the right one sent from the Lord, so Paige's possibility of happily ever after was on hold.

She shook off any despair. "Now, stop slacking off. You left me an SOS note on the bed to come to the hospitality room, once I checked in, and help. I'd checked in, so let's get it done. And where is the local crew?" Paige rested a fist on her hip.

"Putting finishing touches on the banquet room decorations. Others are picking up last-minute items."

There were never enough hands to complete tasks before the ceremony, especially on the first day of the reunion. She wished they'd move the event to another day, but family members said it was too much to have the picnic and banquet on the same day, so every year, it was the same mad rush to arrive early enough for both.

Working side by side, they sorted T-shirts by sizes, then stuffed them in lightweight multi-colored tote bags bearing the family's logo along with snacks and other giveaways for a day at the beach on Saturday.

"How's your friend Dominique?"

"Extremely happy. She got married last weekend and is still on her honeymoon this week." Paige tried to sound upbeat as they got caught up on the happenings in each other's lives over the past year.

"Good for her," Nyla said in a quiet voice.

Soon the double door opened, and another favorite cousin, Claire Blake, entered, setting off another round of screams and hugs.

Daughters of three Blake brothers, they were very close growing up. They spent portions of the summer at their shared grandparents' house in Louisville, Kentucky. Claire and Paige were the same age and took their Christian walk seriously, while Nyla professed to be a Sunday-only Christian.

Now, they had separate lifestyles and goals. Despite their promises of staying in touch throughout the year, family reunions were their quality time together.

"Where's Kenyatta?" Paige inquired about her older cousin and Claire's big sister.

"Randall wanted to go swimming, so my sister probably took him to the pool." The oldest of them all, Kenyatta, was the only one who had married and divorced after two years. Her husband, Lance, had cheated with one of her coworkers. Forgiving and forgetting was too hard, so she had filed for divorce. A month after it was granted, Lance and her former coworker had married. Her cousin had been crushed and scarred for life against any talk about another relationship.

That was a wound Paige never wanted to experience. It made her wonder if Lance had been ready to marry since it didn't take long for his eyes to wander.

"You missed a fine specimen of God's creation," Nyla teased, grinning.

"Who?" Claire asked.

"His name happens to be Blake, and he ain't related. Our dear cousin rode in the elevator with him. I can't imagine how he looks up close and personal. But from down the hall, he was tall and built—definitely maintaining a healthy exercise regimen—great smile with maybe a dimple, close-cropped hair..."

Paige stopped. "And you saw all that from ten or twenty feet?"

Nyla grinned. "When it comes to a man, I have twenty-twenty vision."

"Yep. Nothing's changed with our cousin from last year." Claire chuckled "Is she right?"

"I know nothing about the man." Paige shrugged. Nyla was right about Blake's attributes, except she wasn't sure of the dimple part. Yes, the man was hot, but if he wasn't on fire with the Lord, what was the use taking a second look? She wasn't trying to examine his features. His confident stance probably garnered him all the attention he wanted.

Paige had to remind herself that she was guarding her heart, waiting on God to release it in the hands of a man who would love her forever.

Nyla waved her hand in the air. "Don't worry. Before the weekend is over, I'll know everything about the man, including his credit rating."

Chapter 3

Paige's hazel bedroom eyes made Blake think of…well, the bedroom. When there was a mention of a possible bloodline connection, he shut down any growing attraction. It resurfaced once there was confirmation they were not related.

Their too brief first impression was seared into his mind. Blake couldn't shake, dismiss, or forget the subtle spark that ignited when they shook hands. He needed five more minutes tops to see if there was the slightest interest on her part. Not that he was looking for romance or a relationship so soon, but there was something about her that might change that.

Enthralled with Paige, Blake stayed rooted in his spot and performed a quick assessment of his moving target. Besides her attractive facial features, she had nice long legs, and he estimated her height at five-six or -seven.

What was her story? Was she married, engaged, dating? Did she have children? Where did she live? What did she do for a living? How many siblings? The questions were endless, and he planned to get answers when—not if—their paths crossed over the next three days.

Paige ran away from him without a backward glance—a first. In uniform or in civilian clothes, Blake's good looks always garnered attention from women, whether in the States or overseas. He mused whether she played poker because she gave nothing away about whether she appreciated his assets or not.

Rubbing his face, Blake had to put the thoughts of Paige Blake on temporary hold so he could enjoy his own family gathering. He spun in the opposite direction and continued to the Queen Bee room where his relatives, including the host families, were probably camped out. Blake opened the door without knocking, and all chatter ceased, then the jovial cheers exploded.

"Here comes my big strong nephew, home from the war," said Uncle Harvey, who was teetering on the obese side the last time Blake saw him and had officially crossed over. In his late seventies, he had more weight than hair.

Next came smothering kisses from his fifth cousin Constance and seventh or eighth cousin Jeanie Bell. Elderly cousins were addressed as Aunt or Uncle.

Where were the cousins his age? He wondered as others showered him with hugs, salutes, pats on the back and high praise for his service. This type of attention doled on him by civilians was often humbling. When he put on his uniform, he was doing a job to protect and serve like police officers, doctors, and nurses.

Once the dozen or so relatives finished their hero's welcome, they put him to work. He had been ambushed. Blake arranged tables, then re-arranged them, lugged cartons and boxes from trunks of cars and rode the elevator up and down to their hotel rooms for forgotten items. That task he didn't mind in hopes of running into Paige again.

A few hours later, a text from Tucker, a cousin from Dallas, rescued him from the mission: Arrived. Where you

18

at, cuz? What's your room number?

Blake grinned. Cool. With our kinfolks in the Queen Bee room. Don't come down unless you want to do manual labor. Give me thirty minutes to shower and change. Meet you in the lobby.

He turned back to his relatives with a frown. "Something has come up. I've got to go. See you later."

"Umm-hmm." Aunt Myrtle gave him a side-eye and rolled her mouth. "I bet them other cousins are here. Ain't fooling me. I know y'all thick as thieves." She pointed an arthritic finger at him. "You tell Tucker he better come see me sooner than later."

Laughing, Blake could only nod. Their great-great-something cousin might be in her mid-eighties, but nothing passed under her radar. Her business was to know the family's business. "Yes, ma'am. What gave it away?"

"I don't care if you are grown, you still wear that silly lopsided, crooked Cross smile, especially when you and your cousins are concocting some scheme, then you try and put on an innocent face. Umm-hmm. I didn't have eleven kids and not learn something…and speaking of children, when are you and your cousins getting wives and bringing us another generation…"

Blake was guilty of the scheming but clueless about a wife and family. "I've got time." He kissed her cheek and hurried out the door before he got suckered into an hour-long monologue that he and his cousins had to suffer through as children.

After his quick escape, he glanced down at the other end of the hall. Was Paige still there? He tapped the elevator button and waited to see if she was inside when the doors opened.

She wasn't, so he tapped the third floor. When the doors closed, he sniffed, hoping to detect Paige's fragrance. Nothing. Back in his room, he was about to shower when he caught a glimpse of the wild hairs surrounding his goatee. A touch-up came first. "Never know when our paths will cross," he cautioned his reflection in the mirror. After shaving, he showered, then tweaked his wardrobe. Instead of a T-shirt with his cargo shorts, he chose a cotton short-sleeve shirt with a collar. He slipped on his sandals, grabbed his wallet, and headed out.

Would his heart pound all weekend whenever he waited on an elevator? When the doors opened, three young girls stopped giggling and stared. He greeted them, they blushed and giggled some more. Too bad he didn't have the same effect on Paige.

As soon as he walked out onto the lobby floor, Blake spied his childhood running buddies. It had been at least eight or nine years since he'd last seen everyone. While Blake remained trim, Tucker and the others had thickened up. Some had hair, some didn't. Blake had recently turned thirty-four and planned to keep the waves in his hair as long as he could.

Tucker was thirty-one, but an old soul and wise beyond his years. Neither had brothers, so they treated each other as siblings, and their kinship was unmistakable as relatives. The only difference was they were two different shades of brown—a blend of vanilla and a touch of mocha. Like Aunt Myrtle had said, all first cousins—Crosses and Bells—had the same boyish grin.

"Whatz up, B?" Tucker said, grabbing him in a bear hug.

"Man, it's good to have you back—alive and in one piece," another cousin said.

"You look the same," another cousin commented.

Blake grunted. A wartime soldier never returned home the same, especially knowing roadside bombs could steal a life in minutes.

Tucker clasped his hands. "What are we going to do, stand around here for Aunt Myrtle to come find us, or see what the city has to offer?"

"We're going on the city tour tomorrow," Blake reminded him, knowing his cousin was talking about women sightseeing.

"Yep, but the concierge said we should check out Queology for barbecue and happy hour."

They strolled outside the hotel. The historic area was like a throwback to Small Town USA with its tree-lined streets and narrow sidewalks. Everything was close by. Their destination was five minutes away on foot.

The cousins settled in at the bar and ordered ribs, fries, and drinks.

"Don't think we're not going to get chewed out for being missing in action," Tucker said before he took a swig of his cold drink.

"Hey, I served my time," Blake grunted and shifted his weight on the stool.

"Yeah, I know, in the Middle East and other places on the map."

"I wasn't talking about serving our country, but our family."

Tucker changed the subject. "When your mom told Momma you had been injured, even I started praying."

"Yeah, me too." That was a couple years back. Blake had suffered a severe concussion that caused painful headaches from time to time, but his helmet had saved his life.

21

I saved you. God's voice was adamant.

Blake swallowed and shifted on the stool. *That's what I meant*, he thought.

"How's Cleveland treating you?" Tucker asked, then looked around the place.

"Man, trying to figure out my next move. Don't know if I want to stay there or relocate."

"Dallas has a lot to offer—opportunities, lifestyle—"

"You were gone so long, I was wondering if you were going to make it a career and never come back. What was it like over there?" Before Blake could give his standard glossed-over version of what he preferred to share, Tucker continued, "I mean did you have to kill anybody?"

Blake didn't answer right away. Would civilians ever learn the proper etiquette of conversations with veterans? "Who brags about taking another person's life?"

"Sorry, cuz."

"Forgiven." Blake grinned.

Tucker offered to pay their tab. "Let's see what else is around here."

A couple hours later, back at the hotel, they decided to relax in the lobby and watch out for other relatives who might be checking in.

On second thought, where was Paige and what was she doing? He would pull an all-nighter if he had to so he could see her again. Blake was officially on watch duty.

Chapter 4

Paige surveyed her appearance in the mirror in her hotel as the Blake/Croft family prepared for their evening banquet. She swept up her curls into a ball, then adjusted a faux-crystal tiara on the top of her hair.

"Don't you look like a princess," Nyla said, coming out of the bathroom after artistically applying her makeup.

Patting the crown, Paige thanked her cousin and sat on her bed. "All I need is a prince."

The crown accented the mermaid crystal evening dress Dominique had talked her into buying while they were on the hunt for Dominique's perfect wedding dress. The burgundy was bold compared to the soft colors Paige was known to wear. Plus, it was a bargain. Seeing her transformation, Paige was glad she'd purchased it.

"Don't we all." Removing her bathrobe, Nyla slipped on her after-five dress, which was laid across her bed. Red was her cousin's color, and she was breathtaking in the form-fitting dress, which highlighted her curves. Paige complimented her too, then checked the time. "Will you hurry? I'm ready to see our kinfolks."

Her parents, brothers, their wives, and her four-year-old nephew had taken the scenic route from St. Louis in their cars. They did a couple of stopovers in other places, including Nashville along the way, stretching the twelve-hour ride into days. Since she didn't have enough vacation time, Paige opted to fly in the day of the banquet and ride back with her parents.

"Okay, already," Nyla said, then squinted. "Seriously, in that dress, you're sure to make a grand entrance."

"You do realize we're among family." The elegant attire was for formal pictures taken at the banquet every year to capture families that might not be there the next year. Everyone was expected to dress in their best. The next day, the family would relax at the beach, wearing their Blake/Croft T-shirts.

"You're going to come out of the heels sooner than later, especially after you come down the Soul Train line a couple of times."

"True." Paige chuckled. She wasn't much of a dancer, so the Soul Train line was her limit. Plus, she didn't believe in shaking her butt or other lewd moves in front of family or strangers. The one dance she looked forward to was that first dance with her husband. Until then, she would dance for the Lord, waiting for Him to send another partner.

Finally ready, they grabbed their evening handbags and room keys. They strutted to the elevator as if they were on a runway. The doors opened, and she and Nyla greeted a couple of other relatives who happened to be in the elevator on their way to the ballroom.

The attendance grew every year at the reunions. This time seventy-five families, shy of two hundred folks, were packed inside the ballroom, which was buzzing with activity.

Her cousins, Claire and her sister, Kenyatta, stood from their table and waved. Stopping to chat and hugging relatives, it took her and Nyla a while to reach the seats saved for them.

24

At the adjacent table, their aunt Tuna's eyes lit up. Growing up, Paige thought Tuna was a nickname. Due to a misspelling on the birth certificate, Tina had been Aunt Tuna all Paige's life. "You get prettier every year."

Paige blushed under her compliment. Since she was a little girl, she had a special bond with her father's aunt. Aunt Tuna always shared nuggets of wisdom and scoops of encouragement. She needed whatever her aunt wanted to impart after witnessing her best friend's romantic nuptials.

Her family's table was closer to the front. She smirked, watching her four-year-old nephew Jeffrey spin around with other small cousins. Her oldest brother by seven years, Benjamin, wasn't far away, keeping a watchful eye over his son.

Raymond was next after Benjamin. Paige considered Raymond and his wife, Gina, newlyweds since they had just celebrated their second anniversary. Although her sisters-in-laws, Faith and Gina were sweet, down to earth, gorgeous, and had Paige's back when she needed it. It was nothing like the sisterly bond she had forged with Dominique in high school.

While Benjamin had his wife and son, Raymond had Gina, and they were hoping for a baby soon. Paige was still alone and continued to pray to be a Mrs., sooner than later.

Paige made her way to her parents who were chatting with one of the elders. Her father's eyes lit up, and he opened his arms. "There's my baby girl."

She was used to the childish endearment. She accepted his hug, then kissed him on the cheek, then her uncle Buddy's. "Hi, Daddy."

"You look like your mother, just beautiful!" William Blake beamed, and Uncle Buddy seconded it.

"There you are," her mother, Miranda, said. "Wow, you truly are a princess, sweetie." She patted Paige's crown. Paige blushed over the fuss her parents made over her. "Your prince is coming," her mother added, a spark of hope in her eyes. It was no secret that her family knew Paige longed to be married

"Auntie Paige," Jeffrey yelled.

Turning around, Paige saw her nephew was heading her way. She accepted his hug before he took off again as the organizer, Aunt Trudy, tapped the microphone. "Welcome to the fifty-seventh Blake/Croft family reunion."

The applause was deafening. "If you will take your seats, we'll get this shindig started. Y'all know how this goes. We're going to feast, hand out our recognition awards, take family photos, then we'll let the young people loose on the dance floor."

Cheering exploded from tables where those under thirty had gathered. "I'm asking our own Pastor Gary Cross to ask for blessings over our food."

"With every head bowed," their cousin's deep voice commanded the room. "Father God, in the name of Jesus, thank You for allowing our family to come together one more time. Please bless and sanctify our food, and remove all impurities. Please help us to bless others with nourishment. In Jesus' name."

"Amen" was barely audible when a stampede took off for the buffet tables.

"Hold it," their great-aunt said in the voice of a drill sergeant, and everyone froze. "The elders eat first, so unless you're fixin' them or the little ones a plate, back off from that buffet."

The crowd thinned immediately.

Paige went to prepare a plate for Aunt Tuna, but another cousin beat her to it. Remaining in her seat, Paige waited her turn before she waltzed to one of the four buffet tables. As she inched closer to the food, her father walked up to her.

"You're going to let this old man jump you in line?" His eyes sparkled with mischief.

"Daddy," she said, laughing, "I know Momma has fixed your plate, so why are you trying to get seconds of already?" He pointed to the mashed potatoes. "Go ahead."

He smacked a kiss on her cheek. "You're my favorite daughter."

"I'm your only daughter."

To say she was a daddy's girl was an understatement. If the time ever came that she fell in love with the man who was perfect for her, he would be interrogated by a drill sergeant.

Soft music serenaded them as everyone stuffed themselves with second and third helpings. As the dessert was served, Aunt Trudy, returned to the microphone.

Nyla and another local cousin joined their aunt at the table for the recognition ceremony of every known accomplishment from those who traveled the farthest to anyone who received a job promotion and everything in between. Despite the lengthy process, this was one of Paige's favorite parts of the banquet.

"Cousin Elsie, you're still the oldest reigning queen at ninety-eight," Aunt Trudy said before handing out gift cards to the couple celebrating the longest wedding anniversary, family with most children, grandchildren, great-grands, and newlyweds. In addition to gift cards and plaques, other prizes were given out.

High school and college students received whistles,

standing ovations, and monetary gifts for their grade point averages, scholarships, and degrees. The family believed that showing young people they were important would keep them connected to the family instead of being drawn to fake friends and relationships with bad intentions.

"We have a good name, family. Let's not taint it, but keep doing great things," Aunt Trudy said after all the prizes were handed out. "Now, it's time for this year's family portrait. Bring chairs for the elders to sit on the front row, the smaller ones on the floor in front. Y'all tall folks in the back and the shorter ones in between. So straighten your tie, put on your lipstick, and change those diapers." She chuckled.

Paige didn't envy the professional photographer as he exhausted every effort for cooperation to capture all of her relatives. After the group pose, the photographer moved to a photo booth where everyone from the young children to the teenagers, and even the elders had a blast posing with various funny props.

"Let's go," Claire said, grabbing Paige's hand, following others to the photo booth.

By this time, the DJ started playing familiar jams that enticed the young and old to flock to the dance floor. When the Soul Train line formed, it seemed like Paige glided down the aisle with every family member—her nephew, mom, dad, brothers, sisters-in-law, Claire, and Nyla.

"Feet hurting ya?" Nyla teased as Paige slipped off her stilettos and backed out of the line.

"No. My feet are crying, which is my cue that I could only be a princess for so long." When Paige yawned, she decided to call it a night. "I'll see you in the morning on the beach."

"Okay. I'll hang out down here until Nyla and my sister wear themselves out," Claire said.

If family members weren't on the dance floor, they made trips back to the buffet. The older folks were huddled at tables rehashing old times. Paige wasn't the only party pooper as she trailed others leaving.

She was about to cross the lobby when she heard her name and spun around.

Whipping her neck from side to side, she recognized Blake, the elevator guy from earlier. He was talking to another gentleman.

Both stood and approached her. Somehow, Blake seemed taller and more handsome. "Hi. You look gorgeous."

"Thank you." She accepted the compliment, doubting her princess effect hadn't faded during the banquet.

"Oh, Paige, this is Tucker," he introduced after his cousin cleared his throat.

Smiling, she nodded. "The other family reunion. When does yours start?"

"Tomorrow, bright and early on a tour bus to explore the hidden past of American Black slave history," Blake answered.

"I never heard of it phrased like that."

He grunted and slipped his hands inside his pockets. "America wasn't the only country that enslaved other human beings. We all have our unique history."

"As you can see, our reunion started tonight and goes through Saturday, and we go home on Sunday. It was nice seeing you again and meeting you," she directed at his cousin. She turned toward the elevators. Blake stopped her again.

"It sounds like your party will go for hours. Do you mind keeping me company?"

Eyeing Tucker, she chuckled. "I think you have company."

"Nope. He's just leaving," he said, but it didn't appear Tucker got the message until Blake frowned. Getting the hint, Tucker said goodnight. It was comical.

"See." He smiled, and she realized Nyla had amazingly been right. He did have a dimple. "I could really use some company now." He waved his arm toward the lounge area where he had vacated.

It wasn't like she was going to bed, but she was going to the room to take off her dress and get comfortable. "Sure. We can swap family reunion stories." The sitting area consisted of three oversized chairs—two facing each other—and a third one with a round ottoman in the middle.

After sitting in a banquet chair for hours, Paige sunk into an oversized chair and tamed a purr that tried to escape from her mouth. Resting her shoes by the chair, she wiggled her toes, hidden under her evening gown, then folded her arms.

His eyes sparkled. To say Blake was handsome would be false. He possessed undeniable charisma, yet her heart was on lockdown for the right man—a godly man.

"The Cross/Bell families celebrated their centennial four years ago."

Impressed, Paige blinked, momentarily speechless. Finally, "Wow," stuttered out.

He chuckled. "Yeah. Family members have been meeting every year—whether it's two or two hundred. They refused to cancel the tradition for fear the gatherings would start to wane."

"The Blake/Croft reunion has gotten together for reunions for about fifty-seven years off and on. We're not as dedicated to meet for small numbers, which is why it's been canceled, but when we do come together it's all about family."

Blake nodded and folded his hands. "My dad says gatherings have dated back post-Emancipation where freed African Americans would return to their former enslaved plantations in hopes of finding loved ones that were sold off by cruel men. We don't say slaveholders. We call them capturers.

"So every year, we visit historic sites to remind us of what we've lost and to be appreciative of what we've gained. Reunions to the Cross/Bell family are a serious mandatory family event that is not to be missed, unless you're dead, near death, or like me serving our country."

Knowing he served their country spoke volumes about his character. "Thank you for your service," she said quietly. *Lord, thank You for bringing him and others home safely.* "Hmmm. What branch?"

"I joined the Ohio National Guard. My unit was activated to Iraq, then I enlisted in the army and was sent to Afghanistan. I served three tours and finally called it quits more than a month ago."

She hadn't realized her mind had wandered until voices in the distance jolted her to the present. Had Blake asked her a question because he was staring at her?

Paige resisted the urge to shiver under his scrutiny. She and Dominique were accustomed to catching a man's eye. It was their hearts, they wanted. God had rewarded her friend with a man after His own heart—Dominique got her blessing. Banishing the melancholy, Paige refocused.

31

"I'm sorry, did you ask me something?"

He smiled. "Yes. Where do you live, and what do you do for a living?"

"I'm from St. Louis, and I'm an interior designer. Now that you're back, what do you plan to do?"

"I'm not sure yet."

"So what's on the Bell/Cross agenda, or is it Cross/Bell?" Repositioning in her seat, Paige rested her hands in her lap. Blake's attention to her hands didn't escape her.

"Depending on who you ask it's the Cross—if they're a Cross. Same goes for the Bells. They were blood brothers separated by two slaveholders—Cross and Bell. Our reunion doesn't officially kick off until early tomorrow morning. My family picked South Carolina because of the richness of African-American slavery history in the state like St. Helena Island where the Gullah language still flourishes. That's almost a two-hour ride on the tour bus. We'll see the Aiken-Rhett House of Slave Quarters, Old Slave Mart Museum—that's nearby, and I do want to see that. We'll eat, do a little shopping, then we'll head back for our banquet tomorrow night."

"That's a busy day for a picnic and banquet," Paige said. "Tonight is our big night, so Saturday can be low-key."

Blake nodded. "I guess no two reunions are done the same, but I have to admit, our attire isn't quite as fancy." He scanned her appearance again. "Nice toes and polish, by the way." She quickly tucked her feet under her dress, giggling. "You're one beautiful woman, Paige Blake."

She didn't see that compliment coming, and it left Paige briefly tongue-tied and her heart going crazy. "Thank you," she mumbled, wracking her brain on how to stay on a safe topic. She exhaled when he broke the silence.

"We close out on Sunday with church service." He shrugged and squinted. "A lot of our families are arriving tonight. That's one reason I was hanging out down here, to see them, and I'd hoped to see you." He seemed bashful. "You, Paige Blake, could definitely fit right into my family."

He was smooth. One minute it was about the family reunion, the next he slipped in flattery. She frowned, not knowing where he was going with this. "In what way?"

Linking his hands together, he rested his chin on top of them as he leaned forward. "See that lady over there in the blue at the registration desk?"

Angling her head, Paige couldn't miss her. "You mean that gorgeous woman with the two little girls dressed alike?" When he didn't respond, she faced him again.

He grunted. "I have two older sisters—no brothers. Monique is the oldest. Not trying to brag, but we have pretty women in our family, but you're beautiful with your amazing eyes that don't need sunlight to shine." The awe behind his compliment was so tangible, Paige squirmed in her seat.

Looking for a distraction, she spied more of her family leaving the banquet and a real familiar face. Paige waited until they were in view, then smirked to turn the tables on him. "I have two older brothers. I doubt you could pick them out."

He scanned the lobby and zoomed in. "Found one. The one in the black suit—tall, bearded. I guess that's his son he's carrying."

Her eyes widened in disbelief. "How could you tell?"

"One, he's heading this way with a purpose, and two, he doesn't seem too friendly."

Paige giggled, then stood. So did Blake. He had called it right. Benjamin's body language was stiff and untrusting as he eyed Blake. "I see Jeffrey's knocked out." She patted her nephew's back, stalling to make the introductions just to irritate her brother. "This is Blake Cross."

"Blake," her brother repeated, then relaxed before extending his hand "Family?" A smile tilted his lips.

"Nope." Paige shook her head. "Happens to be his first name instead of our last."

"Oh." He reverted to his hard big brother exterior. "You ready to go up to the room?"

Benjamin had dismissed Blake. He didn't have to be rude. "Nope, not yet," she said, exerting her independence.

She could tell he was gearing up for a comeback when his wife strolled up behind him. Amazingly, Faith was still in her heels. "Hey, Paige." She turned to Blake and lifted an eyebrow. "Hello." She squeezed her husband's arm. "Let's go up, sweetie. We'll see Paige in the morning."

The woman had power over her husband without trying. Paige wondered if she would have the same effect when she got married.

Benjamin grunted with a crooked smile. "Okay. Call me if you need me, sis," he said reluctantly as Faith practically yanked him away.

Returning to their seats, Blake was the first to break the tension with a hearty laugh. "What would we do without family?"

"Trust me, growing up, I wished I could dump them. Now, I respect them."

"No sisters?"

She sighed. "Nope." She thought about Dominique. "I have a good friend who couldn't be closer than a sister. She recently got married."

"Congratulations to her. We have so much in common." He grinned, showing a smile she couldn't ignore.

Paige lifted an eyebrow, waiting for him to clarify.

"We're single." His grin broadened.

"Just because I'm not wearing a ring," she said, recalling him checking out her hand, "doesn't mean I'm not seeing anyone."

Blake twisted his mouth. She could see a challenge coming. "Are you?"

Whoa, she wished she could tell him yes, or that she was close to being engaged, but she had nothing. "No." She never felt more disappointed in her answer.

"Me either." Instead of a look of triumph, his smile was warm. "Besides being the youngest in our families, we're both here celebrating reunions." He paused and gave her a pointed look that drew her in.

She could feel he had more to say, so Paige sucked in her breath and waited him out.

"And you carry one of my names—for now."

Chapter 5

lake just stated the facts as he saw them. Maybe it was too much at one time because she became quiet. "Paige," he called softly, reaching out to touch her hand. On contact, he felt a subtle stir that traveled from his fingertips to his heart. Something was definitely going on with his emotions. Could she not sense it?

He didn't believe in chance meetings. It wasn't a coincidence. When she yawned, Blake wondered if it was a ploy to get away. He wanted five more minutes with her— ten, if she would allow him. "What's on the Blake/Croft agenda for the rest of the reunion?"

Paige seemed to perk up right away. "Tonight was about recognizing family members' achievements. There was also a moment of silence for relatives who have passed on, and we love on our young cousins—love them, love them, love them. It really is a grand occasion. We dress up for a formal family group picture, and all families will get a copy." Although Blake liked her energy, he would cool voicing more admiration. "Tomorrow we'll spend our day at the beach. Saturday night is downtime to shop. Some will go to clubs."

"What about you?" He couldn't keep from being drawn into her sexy eyes.

"I don't have any desire for that type of lifestyle."

He lifted a brow. "What is Paige Blake's lifestyle?"

Another man appeared before she could answer. If he was supposed to be imposing, he held little threat. Blake was trained for combat with or without a weapon.

"Paige, is everything okay? Ben texted me to check on you before I go to my room."

"I'm fine, Ray." She lifted her chin at him. "This is my other brother, Raymond, and this is—"

"I know. Blake Cross. Ben already told me." Ray kept his eyes on Blake as Blake stood to shake hands.

Inches taller than Ray, Blake smirked and gripped his hand with a hearty shake. Ray gave it back to him as if they were arm wrestling. When they broke contact, Blake slipped his hands in his pockets to return his blood circulation. He hoped Raymond was doing the same when his hand disappeared behind his back.

"I can hang down here until you're ready to go up in a minute."

Her brothers weren't subtle in their attempts to make her call it a night.

"How about I'll text you when I get back to my room," Paige said.

Ray seemed to consider her counter offer. "Okay. Make sure to include Dad. He saw you over here, but Mom wouldn't let him interrupt, so he sent Ben a text."

Rolling her eyes, she seemed annoyed. "Good night, Raymond." Both watched as he swaggered to the elevator. Once inside, he kept his eyes locked on them until the doors closed.

"Sorry about the interruption." She smiled, then stifled a yawn. "My brothers can be draining, but I love them."

Blake grunted as he sat again and rested his elbows on his knees. "My sisters' attempts at pampering me are just as annoying—even now at thirty-four. I thought when I grew a mustache that would put an end to them treating me as if I'm still their baby brother."

Paige's lips curled up. "I think Ben and Ray will call me their baby sister, even if I become a grandma." She yawned again.

"Although I have the endurance to sit here all night and take mental notes on everything about you, I can escort you to your room whenever you're ready."

"Thanks, but that won't be necessary." She didn't blink.

He leaned forward and noticed a pin-size mole above her lip. "I'm a gentleman. I received an honorable discharge. I know better than to mess with a woman with two brothers."

She gave him an odd expression. "What makes you say that?"

"As beautiful as you are," he paused and watched her blush, "there's no way your big brothers didn't make sure you know some type of self-defense moves." He winked. "I may be the baby brother, but I made sure my sisters could take care of themselves too."

"True. Plus, I pack a Taser and pepper spray." She grinned and patted her small bag.

He liked her fearlessness and sense of humor. "Now, I'm scared of a pretty woman who packs. Before your brother showed up, you were about to tell me what makes you so unique."

She was quiet as she considered his question, then shrugged. "My lifestyle centers around Jesus. It's important for me to wear the armor of God."

This time, Blake squinted. "Armor?"

38

"Do you read your Bible?"

Well, it wasn't as if he didn't read it. "Yeah."

"Then you might recall Ephesians 6:10–18: *Be strong in the Lord, and in the power of his might. Put on the whole armor of God, that ye may be able to stand against the war strategies of the devil. For we wrestle not against flesh and blood, but against principalities, against powers, against the rulers of the darkness of this world, against spiritual wickedness in high places.* God will give us firm footing. I know soldiers carry guns and ammo, but my shield is bigger and sturdier than any superhero." She chuckled. "I'm a fan of Marvel comic movies."

"Good to know," Blake noted.

"But in verse 16: *Above all, taking the shield of faith, wherewith ye shall be able to quench all the fiery darts of the wicked.* That is a force field of protection around me twenty-four seven. *And take the helmet of salvation, and the sword of the Spirit, which is the word of God.*"

Her energy was combustible. The confidence she had in God was unmatched. He couldn't recall anyone break down scriptures with so much passion and conviction—not even his old pastor. It reminded him of when he had to raise his right hand to affirm the Oath of Enlistment to be in the U.S. Army, since his parents were stern against their children swearing. That edict followed him into the military: *I will support and defend the Constitution of the United States against all enemies, foreign and domestic; that I will bear true faith and allegiance to the same; and that I will obey the orders of the President of the United States and the orders of the officers appointed over me, according to regulations and the Uniform Code of Military Justice. So help me God.* Then there was the Army Values and Soldier's Creed he had to memorize.

Blake meant every word of his pledge, but there was

something about Paige's statement that made him want to join God's army. Odd.

"A military uniform can only fight the wars in this world. My armor can do more damage to the enemy," she said in a way that wasn't offensive as she pointed out the superiority of weaponry. This time when she yawned, Paige stood.

His heart hungered for more as he got to his feet. "Listen, I know it's late, but since neither of us is seeing anyone, I would like us to continue this conversation."

"Just because I'm single doesn't mean I'm available."

"What does that mean?" he asked, walking beside her to the elevator.

"I'm hidden in plain sight until the right man comes along." The doors opened, and they stepped inside. When the door opened on the fifth floor, he got out with her.

"Where do you think you're going? I know this isn't your floor from earlier when you got on." The look she gave him sent a warning to think twice about his answer.

He admired her fierceness. "I'm making sure you get inside your room for the night. I plan to step no farther than the end of the hall."

She nodded. "Good answer." With her shoes dangling in one hand, she scooped up the hem of her dress and lifted her chin in a regal fashion. "Good night, Blake."

"Good night, Paige Blake." Staying rooted in place, he watched her graceful stride with interest. *I want her.*

You have to come through Me to have her, God whispered, frustrating Blake that he was clueless to what the Lord meant.

Too soon, Paige came to her room, even though it was far down the hall. Opening her door, Paige jumped back startled. He readied for action to her rescue. Perhaps an intruder was waiting for her. He wouldn't get her, not on his watch. Busting down doors was business as usual some days in Afghanistan.

Words were exchanged as Blake was about to begin his trek. Paige pointed, then her cousin from earlier stuck her head out in the hall. She grinned and waved frantically. "Night."

Blake chuckled and relaxed. With a salute, he backtracked to the elevator. He couldn't believe that a chance encounter with a beautiful woman had caused his heart to twist in knots.

Was it possible that Paige Blake was the one he couldn't—wouldn't—let get away? He always heard others say that but never thought it would apply to him. Okay, the bedroom eyes were inappropriate with her commitment to Christ, but that didn't lessen his attraction. Her family cartel wouldn't deter him from seeking her out the rest of the weekend, but he guessed praying that God wouldn't get in the way wouldn't help his cause one bit.

Chapter 6

Paige collapsed on her bed without removing her clothes and closed her eyes. Blake was good looking and engaging, but she could hear the voice of God telling her to guard her heart. She didn't have to be told twice.

She opened one eye and spied Nyla tapping away on her phone. "What are you doing?"

"Texting your brothers and my uncle so we both can sleep tonight. You know they will break down this door if they have to." She snickered.

"Right," Paige murmured. She sat up and stretched her legs before standing. She padded across the room to her cousin, so Nyla could unbutton the back of Paige's dress. "I doubt we'll cross paths tomorrow." His name is Blake, she mused. "His family is leaving early to check out historic sites, and tomorrow night is their banquet."

"I wish we had checking out historical sites on our agenda."

"Me too, but I came for the beach. Maybe next year," Paige said. After hanging her dress in the closet, she took one last look at the tiara before removing it. Playing Cinderella was fun. It was almost midnight, so back to reality.

It didn't take long for her to perform her nightly ritual of releasing her beast of curls, brushing them into a wrap, then tying a scarf around her hair. After removing her makeup, she washed her face and applied a night cream. She yawned again as she slipped on a long sleep shirt with *Resting in Jesus* emblazoned across the front.

Nyla was already asleep when she came out the bathroom. Going to her own bed, Paige knelt. "Jesus, You reign. Your will is perfect in heaven, let it be so on earth. Forgive my sins, and help me to forgive others. Thank You for safe travels…" Before ending her prayer, her soul cried out, "Lord, You know I'm lonely, and the devil does too. I don't know if Blake is a decoy or distraction, but keep me from being vulnerable and falling prey to the devil's schemes. I want to be kept," she said, reflecting on Jude 1:24: *Now unto him that is able to keep you from falling, and to present you faultless before the presence of his glory with exceeding joy."*

Being kept was important to her. "In Jesus' name. Amen."

Share My salvation with him, God whispered as Paige climbed in bed. Blake's image appeared as soon as she closed her eyes, and in a second, she had fallen into a blissful slumber.

⋯⋯

"What do you mean you're not going on the historic tour?" Tucker repeated when he called Blake to see what time he was going downstairs for breakfast.

"I'm skipping the bus tour. I'll meet everybody at the Old Slave Mart."

"You're asking for a serious beat down from Aunt

Myrtle, and you should be scared. These history lessons are mandatory for the family."

Blake groaned. "Yes, don't I know it?" He would deal with the tongue lashing later.

"So what's up?"

"I'll explain over breakfast once I know the coast is clear. You know another one of Aunt Myrtle's pet peeves is to be late. I plan to be a little tardy this morning."

"She'll leave us."

"That's the plan." Blake chuckled. See you downstairs at seven-thirty. The bus pulls out at seven."

"Okay. I'll head to the gym first," Tucker said and ended the call.

Instead of the weight room, Blake dropped to the floor to do his daily one hundred pushups. Paige was on his mind when he fell asleep, and again this morning her hazel eyes haunted him awake followed by "*If you want her, you have to go through Me*," which he'd heard that morning.

God was sending him cryptic messages. Good thing church was on the agenda for the next day. He could really use an interpretation at the moment. Checking the nightstand drawer, the old faithful Gideon Bible rested inside. He grabbed it and flipped through the books until he found the passage Paige had mentioned. Blake studied the scriptures for about thirty minutes before he closed the Bible. At face value, he got it, yet Blake sensed there was a deeper message. He pondered what God wanted him to do.

When no clarity came, he performed his daily grooming and dressed. Soon, Blake strolled out of his hotel room. At the elevator, he wondered what his chances were that Paige would be there. When the doors opened, his chances weren't great when others filled the space.

Before he stepped out of the elevator, he looked both ways to make sure the coast was clear of family who were riding the tour bus. He respected his elders, but he had a change of plans. Continuing to do head checks, he crossed the lobby to the Lighthouse Café for breakfast.

Tucker was already helping himself at the buffet bar. A few of his relatives had lagged behind, too, forgoing the tour. One was his elderly cousin Franklin, whom everyone called Uncle Franklin. Seeing Blake, Uncle Franklin's smile stretched across his dark-skinned face. As Blake approached his relatives' table, he watched as Uncle Franklin struggled with his cane to stand and greet him. His two sons who were also seniors had health challenges worse than their father's.

"Hey, there's my soldier." Uncle Franklin gave Blake a hearty embrace, then stepped back. "Welcome home." He gave him a salute, having served in the Vietnam War.

There had been so many conflicts around the world since that controversial war. Unfortunately, current vets from the Iraq, Mosul, Afghanistan, and other Middle East conflicts outnumbered survivors of WWII, Vietnam, and Korean war.

"You know you should be on that bus." He laughed, wagging a naughty finger at Blake. "I ain't scared of Myrtle, but I'm goin' hear about it." He leaned closer. "We ain't scared."

Blake grunted. "Speak for yourself. I remember her spankings as a kid. I figure her old bones are even heavier."

They shared a laugh and chatted a few minutes until Tucker came to the table and spoke.

Blake headed to the buffet. He balanced one plate piled with fruit and the other one with an omelet and pancakes. He looked up to see Tucker making another trip to the smorgasbord. "Did you inhale your food or something?" he joked.

"Growing boy." Tucker patted his stomach.

At the table, his cousin asked, "What's the plan? You know we're down with you, B." He scooped up a serving of scrambled eggs, stuffed them in his mouth, and seemed to swallow without chewing.

"Does this have anything to do with the babe from last night?" Tucker asked with a mischievous grin. "She's hot. Does she have any sisters, cousins, or friends?"

As if Blake could sense Paige's presence, he turned his head, scanning the crowd until he clocked her. There was a bunch of them decked out in brown-and-tan family reunion T-shirts. He smirked. His family's colors were black and tan.

Paige stood out right away. She was laughing, and the sound seemed to float to his ears. He smiled. "You tell me. Here they come now." Stroking his goatee, Blake waited impatiently for Paige to notice him. There had to be about twenty or so people—a mixture of women, children, and a couple of men. When she didn't respond to the vibes he was sending her way, Blake excused himself. He walked up beside her in the buffet line. "Good morning."

She faced him with a surprised expression and smiled.

"Hi, Blake," the woman from last night said in a sing-song tone. "I'm Nyla, another Blake."

She was pretty too with hazel eyes. Another woman bumped Nyla to the side. "I'm Claire Blake." Again, she was another cute one, but it was Paige who held his interest.

"Ladies," he greeted them, then turned his attention back to Paige. "I'll get this for you."

He lifted Paige's fruit plate out of her hand so she could have a firm grip on the plate with hot food.

Tilting her head, she wrinkled her nose in a teasing way. "Thanks, but what are you doing here? I thought you would be gone to the island by now."

"My cousin and I are playing hooky." Blake pointed to his table. Tucker gave a slight nod and wave.

"We thought it might be a perfect day at the beach," he said nonchalantly.

"It's an excellent day for the beach." Nyla winked at Paige, then led the others to a table.

"I thought you were looking forward to the African-American sites," Paige said without skipping a beat at scooping up some scrambled eggs.

"Only one of them." He reminded her of his interest in the Old Slave Mart Museum, which would be his family's last stop. "I was hoping when you get tired of tanning your beautiful skin at the beach, you would want to tag along."

She seemed to give it some thought.

"It's a four-minute walk from the hotel," he added to sweeten the deal.

Looking at him over her shoulder, Paige's hypnotic eyes sparkled. "Only if I can bring family."

"Sure." He could bear the scrutiny of her brothers to be near her. He didn't hide his excitement, and she didn't stifle her amusement. "I guess I'd better let you enjoy your breakfast." As he was about to walk away, he stopped. "By the way, this morning I read that passage you quoted last night."

"Really?" Her face glowed. "Do you mind sitting with me and sharing your thoughts?"

"You don't have to ask twice." He nodded for her to lead the way to her table where there just happened not to be enough room for him, so she snagged a table as close to

47

her cousins as possible. When Blake retrieved his plate, he briefed Tucker. "We're going to the beach. I hope you won't scare anybody in your swim trunks." He laughed and joined Paige.

"Your food is probably cold now from talking with me."

"Soldiers aren't always served hot meals." He had to get accustomed to saying ex-soldier. Blake watched as she quietly said grace. She glanced at him again before forking a strawberry. The woman's features were perfect—from her delicate cheekbones and lashes to the beauty mole.

"As a veteran, I've been conditioned to endure harsh environments, bland food, even…"

"What?" She tilted her head, watching him.

"Putting our lives on the line to pay the ultimate sacrifice." He nodded.

When she didn't say anything, Blake could tell she was thinking, probably mulling over the commitment soldiers make to keep America free.

"Putting your life on the line for others is honorable." She paused and quietly said, "Can I give you the Bible's take?"

"Sure."

"Jesus paid the *ultimate* sacrifice. I can't remember the verses, but I do know it's in Romans 5: *For scarcely for a righteous man will one die: yet peradventure for a good man some would even dare to die. God commends His love toward us, while we were yet sinners, Christ died for us.* That is the ultimate sacrifice, to die for the enemy: us. Jesus just didn't die, He rose again with the promise of an eternal resurrection. Jesus is the ultimate veteran."

He shook his head and released a dry, sarcastic chuckle. "Amazing how you tied that in, but the things I've seen, I can't unsee." *Or the death I've seen with my own eyes.* The last thing he wanted to do was debate her, but the willingness for a regular man to risk his life to defend others was an ultimate sacrifice. He thought about one private first class.

I was there, God whispered, *when John Kassel died. I was there.*

You were? That spooked Blake that he hadn't mentioned John's name, but God knew. Why John? They had been the same age when his friend was killed. To Blake, John had died alone, away from family, friends, and even his fellow soldiers who found him. His heart pricked with sorrow, which caused him to pick at his omelet before taste-testing it. It was cold. He could man up and devour it as he had boasted to Paige or get a fresh one because he was no longer on active duty and could indulge in a hot, tasty dish.

"If my hope, joy, and peace is only limited to this world, the Bible says we are most miserable. And the hopeless are the ones who bring darkness into our lives and death. That's why I constantly read and study my Bible, to encourage myself when I see things I can't forget." She became quiet, and once again, he could tell something was pulling at her.

Active combat could haunt veterans for the rest of their lives, but what was haunting Paige, especially with the great faith she professed? He wanted to crack her code, and it would start at the beach.

Chapter 7

Paige liked Blake. At first, she thought he was trying to hit on her. Her brothers said that's what men do when they see a good-looking chick, whether they were sincere in their motives or not. What was endearing was he had read his Bible because of something she said. While some would say, "Only what you do for Christ will last," Paige preferred to quote First Corinthians 1:58: *Therefore, my beloved brethren, be steadfast, unmovable, always abounding in the work of the Lord. Know that your labor is not in vain in the Lord.*

After breakfast, her cousins seemed excited about Blake's cousin tagging along. While Nyla and Claire added lipstick and blush to their appearance, Paige did the opposite. She applied sunscreen, grabbed her glasses and floppy hat and was ready to go.

Once the Blake and Croft families arrived on the beach, nestled between the Folly River and the Atlantic Ocean, everyone seemed to scatter for their favorite water activity.

"Come on, let's get a volleyball game started," Paige shouted to idle family members.

"Got room for more?" Tucker, Blake's cousin, appeared from nowhere.

She immediately craned her neck for Blake. He waved at her from the sideline.

The first game was lively, entertaining, and a workout, but the other team with Tucker won. After a five-minute break, Paige's team returned to even the score. They lost again. She threw up her hands in defeat. "I'm done."

"You're not going down like that," Blake said, coming to her side.

"I'm exhausted." Paige put her hands on her hips and tried to catch her breath. She definitely was out of shape. "I can't. Team Croft won."

"Hey, I have to redeem my name." He took off his T-shirt, and Paige had to look the other way to keep from drooling. Wow. Kudos to his Sculptor. Blake corralled enough Blake and Croft men to form their own teams and the women watched. Before it was over, the Blakes had tied the wins two and two.

The Crofts begged for one more game to declare a champion, but Blake didn't take the bait. Grabbing his shirt, he wiped the sweat off his face and neck before slipping it back on.

Paige couldn't resist squirting a bottle of water at him. She laughed as he chased her across the beach, but didn't retaliate. "I know how women are about their hair."

"So why didn't you accept the challenge from my cousins?" Folding his arms, Blake flexed his biceps. "I played to even the score. It wouldn't seem right to beat your cousins in a game meant for family. If we won three, the Crofts would have cried foul. If we lost, the Blakes would have blamed it on Tucker and me." She liked his reasoning.

"Now, how about joining me on the tour of the Old Slave Mart Museum?"

51

"I would like to, but the tour bus won't be back for a couple of hours."

"We can order an Uber ride back," he countered.

Paige and her cousins rode back with the two men. They agreed to shower and change. They would meet up in the lobby in an hour for the museum. In her hotel suite, Nyla showered first, then Paige. The humidity had danced in her hair until there wasn't much she could do but brush it into a bushy ponytail.

"That was fun," Nyla said, surveying her lipstick.

"And exhausting." Paige stepped into her sundress, then called Claire.

"Go on and have a good time. I need a nap." She yawned and disconnected.

"Looks like it's me and you, cuz," Paige said.

Nyla grinned, "Yes." The cousins never competed with men. Whether Claire was attracted to Tucker or not, she bowed out.

On their way to the elevator, Nyla said, "Blake likes you."

Tilting her head, Paige smiled. "Hmm. I think I know that, but don't think I didn't see how you and Tucker hit it off."

"I have no problem admitting, Tucker is fit and fine, and I wouldn't mind getting to know him better." She wagged her finger. "But back to you. *I* think you'd better not dismiss Blake's intentions. Didn't you say Dominique met Ashton when he was delivering a package to her? Consider an elevator your chance meeting. You can only go up," Nyla stated.

"If he's sanctified for God's purpose. If not, the devil would rather take Blake down to the pit with him. I don't

plan to go there over a man." *God, You can keep me from falling.*
Guard your heart, God whispered from Proverbs 4:23.
Exactly how would she do that around Blake Cross?

"Gorgeous," Blake whispered from his viewpoint across the lobby with Tucker nearby. He couldn't keep from smiling as he observed Paige and Nyla exiting the elevator. She had an unassuming poise about her that attracted men. If they'd get a glimpse into her smoky hazel eyes, they would be a goner—like him.

It seemed like Paige had been settled in Blake's heart for a lifetime instead of less than twenty-four hours and counting. One thing was for sure: This weekend wouldn't be enough for him.

"Hey." They exchanged smiles when she stood in front of him. She looked and smelled equally fresh. "You clean up good." He grinned, and she sniffed.

"You too," she teased back.

"Let's go." He had preferred to walk the short distance, but for the ladies' sake and because of the heat, they took a taxi.

Literally seconds later, the four of them stepped out of the cab and onto the cobblestone street and stared at the Gothic building that was a remnant of horrific American history. Blake could only imagine the sorrow that took place once people walked under the archway where it turned into an American slave castle like the ones in Africa.

Above the entrance, MART was etched into stone. Beneath it, the OLD SLAVE MART MUSEUM wording was worn and faded.

After visiting so many historical sites pertaining to African American slavery since he was a child, Blake wasn't expecting the Old Slave Mart on Chalmers Street to be so in your face and preserved throughout time. Hidden in plain sight, the architecture blended with neighboring structure, squeezed between coiffure homes and other buildings that carried on business as usual. And the Old Slave Mart was thriving business for domestic human trafficking after the United States put a ban on international enslaved trade in 1808.

"Are we going inside, or are we going to stand out here?" Tucker broke into his reverie.

"Yeah." Blake paid the cheap admission fee for himself and Paige, then cautiously entered hallowed ground. The small space was a stark contrast to the façade. Exposed brick and fractured concrete floors were the backdrop to the renovated part that displayed replicas of the past.

Scanning the literature, the four-story building had a kitchen where slaves cooked, a jail where they were imprisoned, and a morgue for their remains called a dead house. Ryan & Sons Mart was the only surviving slave auction gallery in South Carolina. Next to it was a picture of an auction table to showcase enslaved Blacks for sale.

Staying close to Paige, Blake heard her breath catch as she read a flyer that advertised an 1856 estate sale for a "Gang of 67 Negroes" for house servants. "How sad." Her whispered voice cracked. Bowing her head, she shook it from side to side.

"Yes," he said. "This is America's history."

"I know. My family didn't get our hazel eyes from native Africans. It's a European trait. Walking a few paces ahead, she whispered, reading another slave auction at Ryan &

Sons Mart, "*A gang of 25 Sea Island Cotton and Rice Negroes.*"

They stopped at every exhibit before wandering outside to a courtyard cemetery of sorts.

"You okay?" He faced her.

"No." She took a deep breath to add life to her dazed expression. If only he had the liberty to wrap her in his arms for comfort—for both of them. After noting numerous headstones along the pathway, they decided to backtrack inside and see if Tucker and Nyla were ready to go. Blake froze. "*Uh-oh.*"

"What's wrong?" Paige looked at him with worry in her eyes.

"You see that mob of people in there? That's my family. This is their last historic stop before going back to the hotel, and that old woman tapping her cane on the ground and pointing at me is Aunt Myrtle."

"Busted." Laughter spilled out of Paige's mouth.

She didn't know Aunt Myrtle would release her tongue lashing on him as if he was thirteen again—and in front of a woman he wanted to impress. Not good.

"Come on. We might as well face the music." He guided Paige toward his elder.

Paige elbowed him. "Speak for yourself. Your aunt is after you, not me." She didn't hide her amusement. "As a matter of fact, let me find Nyla and we can meet you back at the hotel."

Without thinking, Blake reached out and grabbed her hand to stop her from fleeing. Sparks flew, judging from the confused expression on Paige's face before she shook herself free, she felt them too.

Chapter 8

"Whew," was the only thing Paige could utter once alone back in her hotel room. Nyla was missing in action, either she was with Tucker or their other cousins. Either way, Paige welcomed the solitude. Her attraction to Blake scared her, and she didn't know what to do about her emotions. This was when she needed Dominique to talk sense into her.

While Blake and his family were gearing up for their banquet, the Blake/Croft reunion was winding down. The hospitality room was set up for trivia, video, board, and kiddie games. Shoppers only had to walk across the street to the marketplace.

After a short nap, which was an hour longer than she planned, Paige quickly freshened up and left her hotel suite. Passing by a window overlooking the Palmetto Courtyard, she did a double take and backed up. The courtyard had been transformed for a fairytale wedding. A string of clear lights crisscrossed from the buildings high above the rows of chairs. Touching the window, she felt like a little girl peeping inside a dollhouse, wanting to be on the other side in the bride's shoes.

Closing her eyes, she willed herself to walk away. Once she reached the lobby, curiosity—or stupidity—led her outside on the veranda with other curious hotel guests. Why was she subjecting herself to this?

God had told her to guard her heart. How long? The groom, decked out in a military uniform, and his groomsmen entered the courtyard. He wore the identical expression Ashton had when he married her best friend—the anticipation of forever happiness.

It had hurt like crazy to crave her friend's jubilation from afar. They had always hoped they would find love together—brothers, friends, or coworkers. She sniffed. God had forsaken her. Would a man's heart ever be filled with that much love for her? Moisture in her eyes made Paige blink.

The flower girl appeared to the audience's *ooh*s and *ahh*s. She reminded Paige of a ballerina with her blond curls captured in a tiara similar to the one Paige had worn the evening before at the banquet. Finally, the bride appeared, escorted by her father. The white wedding dress was almost blinding against the darkening sky. *Lord, stir my husband's heart to find me.*

More tears fell. Paige had seen enough. Her emotions were too raw to head to the hospitality room to play games. She would hide in her room and welcome a cleansing cry.

"A lieutenant colonel takes a bride." Blake's deep voice from behind her sent chills down her arms.

There was no way anyone was going to see her like this. She discreetly sniffed to hide her sorrow, and his cologne filled her senses. Not good. She dabbed at her eyes and blinked away tear residue clinging to her lashes. Blake's handsome face came into view as his closeness invaded her private space. He cleaned up well with a crisp long-sleeve shirt, dinner jacket, and slacks.

"Paige, are you okay?"

No wouldn't come out as he placed his hand on her back and guided her inside the hotel. He didn't stop moving until they were back at the same spot as the night before. Her life seemed to be turning into a series of déjà vu.

Stupid question. The woman was crying. Something had shaken this strong woman of faith, and he wanted to know what.

Before he could open his mouth and repeat the question, she blurted out, "I don't want to talk about it."

O-okay. He didn't press her. He took a few minutes to admire her. There hadn't been a moment this weekend when she didn't look beautiful. The first time, her mass of glistening curls, her seductive hazel eyes, and her delicate features had arrested his senses. Last night, she resembled an heir to royalty. The wild hair as a result of the beach was alluring, and now, the simple long, bushy ponytail and casual attire did nothing to hide her beauty.

"So what should we talk about, Miss Blake?" He liked sharing his name with her.

Her eyes seemed to stare past him before meeting his. She scanned his attire and smiled. "You look nice. Coming from or going to your banquet?"

"Taking a break." He wasn't about to tell her he was heading to his room for…he couldn't remember what for. His intention to return to the banquet was now void. "We've already eaten, so I—"

"What was on the menu?" she asked unexpectedly.

Was this her way of avoiding whatever saddened her?

58

"The boring stuff is going on now if you ask me. The elders have been researching our ancestry ever since I can remember. Right now, they're reading the names of the families on the tree. As you can imagine, hearing this every year is a lengthy process, and most of us can recite the tree in our sleep."

She folded her hands. "In the Old Testament, the Levi priests used to gather the Jewish people and read the Law of Moses. It was considered a sacred time…" She drifted off, then bounced back. "So you can recite people, places, and children on your family tree?"

She was coming back to life—good—but he was still concerned. To nurture the light that was returning to her eyes, he would play along. "All nine hundred and seventy-eight descendants of Jake Cross and Sherman Bell? I can't."

When her jaw dropped in surprise, he grinned. He had succeeded in distracting her from some haunting unpleasant memories.

"Kiddin'. Children who are old enough to attend school are expected to learn about their genealogy. Our families don't trust school systems to teach accurate information about the American Black experience, so the family reunions serve as a time to fill in the gaps and usually take place in historic cities. It's a reminder to the next generations of the hardships of our enslaved descendants and the sacrifices they made for what we take for granted today at times. Those who died had paid an ultimate sacrifice too…" He paused and leaned forward, baiting her to fill in the blanks with him. "Not like Jesus," they said in unison.

"See, I catch on fast." He winked, and she blushed. "Back to my family. Jake and Sherman Gaillard were twins

59

and young when their sisters—five in all—were sold off. They remembered Dinah was the last to go. The family reunions began twenty years after the Emancipation Proclamation on the McLeod Plantation. To this day, none of those sisters' descendants have been recovered. One possibility is the common thread that their enslavers raped them and the descendants passed as white, but our elders will stay on the hunt."

"America's history is so sad," she whispered, then smiled. "You are a fascinating person."

"And you are a beautiful woman—spiritually and physically. I'm glad we met."

"Me too. So tell me more." She shifted in the chair and tucked her feet under her bottom. It was apparent she didn't want to talk about herself.

He could talk to her all night—every night. "By the time they were fifteen, Jake was sold to Crawford Cross to pay off the enslaver's debt. His brother was willed to Franklin Bell. Both men had ten children. Their children had seven. Twins popped up every now and then. The brothers' descendants had been separated to Nebraska, Oregon, and Texas… When freedom was declared, many moved up north to Boston where they hoped the life of a freed black would be void of prejudices. It wasn't."

Although Paige didn't interrupt, her hazel eyes were expressive. A few times they misted from the pain of slavery, so he would lighten the mood. "Tomorrow, our tradition calls for an early breakfast, then church service before we go our separate ways. Again, this is mandatory."

"I like the richness and commitment of your family ties."

"What about me?" He feigned a teasing pout.

"You're okay too."

He covered his chest. "I'm wounded. Please come with me."

"My immediate family, a few others, and I usually try to attend a Bible teaching church service before we hit the road, if our host family doesn't have it on the program, so we're going somewhere in the morning. I can use some Godly inspiration."

And I can use some Godly direction. Blake thought that was a good lead-in to her opening up about her tears. She didn't. Maybe he was reading too much into it. Didn't women cry at weddings? He would double-check with his sisters. "Can I ask you a question?" She nodded, so he proceeded. "Earlier you said you weren't available until the right person came along. What if he has arrived?"

She lifted an eyebrow in a challenge. "Trust me. I'd know."

Her confidence intrigued him. "How?"

"Our hearts would beat as one."

Stretching out his legs, he linked his hands together behind his head. His heart started racing the moment he first saw her. What about hers, or was she playing hard to get?

Suddenly, his mother appeared, and his dad was not far behind her. "So this is where you've been hiding," she said in a teasing scold, frowning at him and smiling at Paige.

"Not hiding. We're in plain sight," he borrowed a phrase from Paige as he introduced her.

His mother blinked. "Blake?" she said, then smirked. "I like that name too."

They exchanged a few pleasantries before Paige announced she'd better head to her room against his protest. "Nice meeting you, Mr. and Mrs. Cross."

Before she escaped, he needed her commitment to see her again. "You're coming to church in the morning with me, right?"

"It's possible." Her smile was bright.

"Good night, dear," his mother said, and they watched her disappear into the elevator without looking back.

Lily Cross spun around and stared at him. "I like her."

"Me too." He folded his arms, wishing his parents hadn't shown up.

"So what are you going to do about her, son?" His father gave him an odd expression as they turned to go to their rooms.

"Go after her with all the ammo I've got," he said with feigned confidence. Blake had no idea what kind of arsenal it would take to win the battle for her heart.

Chapter 9

one? Blake's heart plummeted when he called the front desk to be connected to Paige's room Sunday morning only to learn she had already checked out.

Rubbing his hand over his shaved face, he chided himself for not asking for her number last night or giving her the name of the church the Bell/Cross family was attending. The disappointment stayed in the pit of his stomach as he dressed and while he packed his bags.

Blake refused to part ways without a goodbye, even if he had to drive to St. Louis to get it. Closing the door to his suite, he made his way to the elevator. What were the odds she would be inside when the doors opened? The odds were against him again as he crammed into the crowded space with other guests and their luggage, minus Paige.

The lobby area was a frenzy with folks checking out, saying goodbyes, and…Paige. His upset stomach settled, and his spirits lifted. She sat quietly in a nook close to the registration counter. As he rolled his suitcase toward her, she seemed content, almost peaceful, despite the buzz around her. She was reading her Bible.

Today, Blake would describe her as dainty, wearing a long blue-and-green skirt and a fancy blouse. Her pretty toes peeped out from her shoes.

"Hey. Good morning." Would her eyes tell him what she

63

wouldn't—if everything was okay? "I thought you'd left me." He twisted his lips into a pout. "I called your room."

She stood, and her perfume stirred the space between them. "Sorry. We checked out for the family send-off meeting with breakfast. Since you didn't tell me what time the service started or where the church was, I thought I'd wait until you came downstairs. I figured I wouldn't miss you from this spot."

She hadn't seen him coming. Blake had seen her first. All that mattered was she was there. "I see you're getting a jumpstart on the sermon." He pointed to the Bible.

"I was reading my daily inspiration." She hugged the Bible to her chest. "Philippians four, verses seven and eight."

Clearly, her relationship with the Lord was tangible, and he craved…what? He didn't even know. "Can you quote them?"

"*The peace of God, which surpasses all understanding, will guard your hearts and your minds in Christ Jesus.* Amen."

"Amen." He smiled. Why did the scriptures sound better coming from her? "Let me find my parents. I know there's room in our car."

"She won't need a ride," a recognizable voice said from behind him.

Blake pivoted on his heel. "Excuse me?" Why wasn't he surprised by Ben's presence?

"Our family never passes up an invitation to church. We're all coming."

Lifting an eyebrow, Blake asked, "How many is 'we'?"

"Oh," Ben paused and tilted his head from side to side as if he was doing a calculation. "About ten carloads."

What? Blake exhaled. "Okay." So much for an intimate

inspirational parting of ways. But where there was a will, Blake would find a way for a private moment.

Paige glanced in the rearview mirror. As the designated driver, following a GPS to the address Blake had given her, she led the pack of cars with her family members to Jesus' Redemption Power Church twenty minutes away from the hotel.

In no time, she pulled into the church's packed parking lot. An attendant approached wearing an orange safety vest. "There's an overflow lot." He pointed ahead, and she followed his directions.

The parking wasn't much better, but she and her family found sporadic available spaces. Getting out, they waited until they were all together.

"There's at least thirty of us. I hope there's room for us to sit together," her mother said, voicing her concern.

"With all these vehicles, I doubt that's a possibility," Paige said, walking ahead of them. Ushers greeted them with "Praise the Lord" as they entered the building.

Ahh. She was at home. Paige heard her name and spun around. So did her relatives.

Blake's confident gait brought him to her in a few strides. "We have space."

"For all of us?" her mother asked, fanning her arm toward the family behind her.

He grinned that wide smile. "Yep. I asked the usher to reserve four extra rows for our family reunion."

"I like him," her mother stated, and others agreed.

Paige smiled. Blake had earned a brownie point. They

trailed him into the sanctuary where praise and worship filled the atmosphere. Sure enough, somehow, there was a pocket of empty space squeezed out by crowded pews. Paige estimated the membership easily at three thousand, with another thousand folks possibly in an overflow area. When she scooted into a pew, Blake was right behind her.

She frowned and chuckled. "Aren't you going to sit with your family?"

"I'm within the perimeter."

"Funny." She got on her knees and gave thanks for standing on holy ground, then stood to join others in worship. Blake got to his feet, too, and whether intentionally are not, he clapped off beat. "Where's your rhythm, black man?"

"You throw me off," he whispered.

Paige squinted. Why did that sound like he was talking about more than his rhythm? The segment concluded with a moment of applause for the Lord.

Soon, the church's pastor, Elder Jeremiah Malcomb, stood at the podium. "Welcome visitors. I understand we have members from a family reunion here." He glanced down at cards. "No, two. Will the Crosses and Bells stand?"

Paige's wow never made it out of her mouth as Blake stood rows behind members of his family, which had to number in what looked like a hundred people. The crowd gave them a hearty applause. She swallowed. Her family was about to pale in comparison.

"Now, will the Blake and Croft family stand."

The congregation gave them the same applause. Once they took their seats, her brother Benjamin leaned over between her shoulder and Blake's. "We'll beat you next time."

Next time? Really? There wouldn't be a next time. Paige rolled her eyes. She knew her brother had a competitive spirit, but in church?

"I look forward to a rematch." Blake took the bait.

"If you will open your Bibles to Matthew twenty-five. I'm going to read the first ten verses, but the message will come from verse ten…"

"Will you share your Bible with me?" Blake whispered.

"The verses are on the overhead screen," Benjamin butted in.

This time, Paige turned around and gave her brother a stare inherited straight from their mother.

Pastor Malcomb ended with verse ten: *"'And while they went to buy, the bridegroom came; and they that were ready went in with him to the marriage: and the door was shut.'* My sermon today is a question: Are You Ready?" He paused. "How many of you have been invited to a wedding recently?"

Paige's shoulders slumped. If the minister stuck with Christ's spiritual wedding, she could handle it. Otherwise, the subject was off the table in her current state of mind.

Blake's hand covered hers, and he squeezed. His touch seemed to singe her skin. Without facing him, Paige slowly removed it.

"Weddings happen every day, and invitations are not extended to everybody. There's a guest list, and well, if you're not on it, you're turned away. We've all experienced the moment where doors are shut on us—whether a job, relationship, or other opportunities."

Don't cry. Don't even sniff, she coaxed herself at the thought of God shutting the door on her in regards to love.

"The good news is," Elder Malcomb continued, "Jesus is issuing an open invitation to people to His wedding feast." He raised his voice. "Here's something else that's free: the Holy Ghost, which represents the oil in the lamp. The virgins were shut out because they didn't have enough of what Christ freely gives. This is a heavenly celebration, your ticket is the Holy Ghost, and your salvation walk isn't complete without it. You only need to repent. You may not want to recall the things you've done in the dark, but trust me, God has brought them to light…"

The man preached with the power of God's anointing until folks were on their feet, including members of both family reunions, cheering him on. His sermon ended too soon.

"It's invitation time. God's salvation is easy: repent. Don't let the rapture come and you be shut out of God's glory. This is the altar call. Please stand." He paused. "If you know in your heart you haven't surrendered your life to Christ, come. Repent of your sins. I'm not going to coach you on what to say. I don't know what is in your heart. God does. Let His blood wash your sins away in the water baptism in Jesus' name. Once you're redeemed with His Blood, He wants to freely give you fresh oil, which is the Holy Ghost. The evidence He gave us is to hear heavenly tongues flow from our mouths as Jesus speaks… Come."

With her eyes closed, Paige prayed silently for souls to take heed. Where was Blake in his salvation walk? She'd never asked. Leaning closer, she looked at him and whispered, "Have you repented and received the water and Holy Ghost baptism in Jesus' name?"

He blinked his soulful eyes. "I was baptized when I was a boy."

"You're a man now. Have you strengthened your salvation walk?" More questions filled her head, but she kept silent as the shepherd of the house ministered to lost souls.

After the service, her family introduced themselves to Blake's while he pulled her aside. "There is an attraction between us, maybe more on my part," he paused as if he was waiting for her response. When she didn't respond, he continued, "I want us to keep in touch. Good things could happen between a Blake and Blake."

She chuckled at his silliness to shake off the fluttering in her heart. "I don't think it's a good idea to try and pursue a relationship."

"Because you're in St. Louis and I'm in Cleveland?"

"It's not the physical distance that concerns me, but the spiritual. Where are you in your relationship with Christ? Do you talk to Him and listen when He talks back?" She softened her tone. "I don't want a relationship with a man I can't trust to lead me—"

"I was in charge—"

She held up her hands. "I'm not talking about troops in the military," she said, shaking her head. "I want to close my eyes, be blindfolded and take my husband's hand because I trust him to lead as Christ gives him directions."

Blake whistled. "Talk about putting pressure on a brother."

"See," she said, shrugging, "if a man can love God without pressure, he can love me—his wife—and not feel pressured to give me his love."

The expressions that crossed his face were unreadable. She could only pray he would bounce back after her rejection. She really did like him as a person and wasn't trying to hurt him. "Let's just end it here, okay?"

Shaking his head, he folded his arms. "That's not okay."

"Sorry." Her heart ached for hurting him.

He unfolded his arms and held them open. "Can I at least get a goodbye hug?"

"Of course." She stepped into his arms and inhaled his cologne, then stepped back. "Have a safe trip home."

She didn't exhale until she was behind the wheel of her father's car.

After waving to other family members, she pulled behind Benjamin who had the motor running and was waiting on her. Raymond sandwiched her in as they began the thirteen-hour trip home.

"Do you like him?" her mother asked when they exited on the interstate.

"Yes." She would never forget him.

"Do you plan to keep in touch?" her father asked.

"No."

There was no further discussion of her and Blake Cross.

Chapter 10

What did I say? Blake replayed his conversation with Paige as he stared out of the plane's window. Unlike most of his family who drove home, Blake opted to fly back to Cleveland.

How could she say no to him? Whether Paige admitted it or not, they connected. They were attracted to each other. It wasn't one-sided. Paige confided in him—well, a little— but that was like bribing a toddler with a toy when she was under distress. How could she not trust him?

Do you trust Me? God whispered.

Blake blinked and held his breath. Of course, he trusted God. Who didn't?

If you had trusted Me, then you would have given Me all the praise, God said.

I'm sorry, Blake silently said as he bowed his head, confused. What did any of this have to do with Paige?

"Sir, would you like anything to drink? Sir?" The flight attendant interrupted his musings.

"No, thanks." Why did God have a beef with him?

A man asks the father's permission for his daughter's hand in marriage. Paige is My daughter. God cited passages in the Bible that he would have to search.

Marriage? Commitment was the farthest thing from his

71

mind when he returned home from Afghanistan. That was before he felt something special over the weekend with Paige. There was a possibility Paige could be the one, but how would he know for sure if she didn't want to talk to him, and God had set up perimeters around her—a spiritual cartel?

Closing his eyes, Blake rested his head on the back of the seat. His father drilled into his head when he joined the Ohio National Guard, "Finish what you start." He planned to do just that with Paige.

⤝⤜⬦⤞⤟

No, he didn't. Paige didn't know if she should be flattered, annoyed, or a mixture of both as she stared at the Facebook friend request from Blake on her phone.

It wasn't the first time that a handsome man pursued her, but she effortlessly held them at bay with the Word of God. Knowing the consequences of sin made Paige more determined not to tempt her hormones.

Blake had the looks, charisma, and confidence, but where was God in his life—first, second, third, or runner-up when he was in trouble? Paige wanted a godly man, a praying man, a faithful man. Where was he already?

"Ready to eat?" her father asked. After so many hours on the road, her family had checked into a Nashville hotel. They would stay overnight and continue home in the morning.

"If you're treating, Daddy, I'm eating." She grinned, meeting the same hazel eyes he had passed down to her.

Let Blake Cross stew, she decided. Why couldn't he walk away and chalk it up to a great weekend? Even promises with her cousins to keep in touch always fizzled once they returned home. A few phone chats with Nyla and Claire throughout the year—if that—was all they managed to squeeze in with life's other commitments. There was no place in her life to give Blake without a green light from the Lord.

Grabbing her purse and door key, the family squeezed into the elevator. She chuckled.

"What's funny?" Benjamin asked, holding onto his son's hand.

"Just thought of something," she said, thinking how she and Blake had met with a misunderstanding in an elevator. She chuckled again to Benjamin's raised eyebrow.

Once in the lobby, they strolled outside toward O'Charley's Restaurant & Bar. For the next hour, they shared highlights of the reunion and discussed what city would host the event the following year.

"I hope the next hotel won't book two family reunions again. It was a madhouse," Benjamin stated.

Faith nudged her husband. "It wasn't that bad, except at checkout."

And I met Blake who is now waiting to be my Facebook friend.

The next day, on Monday afternoon, her father parked in front of the family home where she had left her car. After transferring her luggage and things from his car to hers, she exchanged hugs, kisses, and declarations of love then headed to her apartment near the Washington University-St. Louis campus.

It felt good to have her own place again. Not long ago, she had lost her job and had to move back home. Her family was happy to have her, but Paige felt like a loser and made up her mind the next time she moved out, she didn't plan to come back. Eight months ago, she had landed a position as an interior designer at the prestigious Safe Style Designs. Although she felt her job was secure, she saved more than she spent.

Three months ago, she'd signed a one-year lease with her spacious apartment. Her neighborhood was picturesque with colorful vibrant flowerbeds leading to the grand entrance, in contrast to the water-thirsty lawns as a result of the summer heat.

Her routine was back to normal: long hours at work, Bible class on Wednesday, singles ministry for Friday, and morning worship on Sunday. The weekends had always been her time with Dominique to do things together. Not anymore. There was no one to fill the void.

From here out, Paige would attend the singles ministry without her sidekick. At least her best friend would return from her honeymoon next Saturday. Did the couple visit the sites she and Dominique had planned to scope out? Her questions were endless. Paige couldn't wait to hug Dominique.

For the rest of the week, work projects consumed Paige. When she had breathing room, she thought about Blake V. Cross Jr. waiting in the wings for her to accept his Facebook friendship. She wondered what the V stood for—Vance, Victor, or some traditional family name. When she searched for Blake Cross, there were dozens. Why was this such a difficult decision? The only requests she rejected were spams. Otherwise, she knew everyone she friended.

Thursday night, while on her knees before bed, she ended her prayer, "Lord, You said in Proverbs 3:6 to acknowledge You in all my ways and You will direct my path. Jesus, You told me to guard my heart. I've done that to the best of my ability." She asked if Blake was a threat or whether she was making a big deal about nothing. She listened, but God was silent.

Friday evening, as Paige rushed home from work to get ready for the weekly singles service, Nyla called her.

"Have you talked to Blake?"

Paige stopped what she was doing. "Well, hello to you, too, cousin. No. Why?"

Nyla laughed. "Tucker and I have been FaceTiming each other since we left Charleston. He's flying in from Dallas in the morning for breakfast. Romantic, huh?"

Paige blinked and flopped on the bed. "I don't know if that's romantic or heartbreak." She gnawed on her lips in contemplation. "I mean, you two just met, and he's moving fast."

"Don't hate because Blake is slow."

Trust me, the man is anything but that. Paige withheld her smirk. He had sent a friend request within two hours of them saying goodbye. If anybody was slow, it was Paige.

"Be careful, cousin. Long-distance relationships don't have good track records."

"Right," Nyla snapped with an attitude, then changed the subject. "So what are you doing tonight?"

Playing it safe. "Going to my church's Friday night singles ministry."

"I'm sure that will be memorable," Nyla said sarcastically. "No wonder you and Claire have yet to meet Mr. Right."

"Umm-hmm." Paige wasn't going to take the bait. "I've got to finish getting ready." After they disconnected, she prayed for her cousin who was on the fast track of securing a husband.

Soon, Paige entered the chapel at Salvation Temple. Stepping into her usual pew, Paige knelt, gave thanks for being in God's presence, then prayed for herself in the love department.

Minister Quinton Ray, a newlywed himself, remained the group leader. His wife, Mya, was his assistant and a source of spiritual encouragement to the sisters.

"Praise the Lord, everybody." He stood before the gathering of about fifty saints. "Since it's mid-August and we're getting a break from the humidity for the next couple of days, I thought we could enjoy cool treats on the side parking lot after we're finished tonight. I've invited some of our sister churches to stop by after their service to fellowship."

After a chorus of "Amens," he directed everyone to a familiar scripture, Ecclesiastes 3:1: *To everything there is a season, and a time to every purpose under the heaven.* As summer comes to a close, let's look to what God has in store for us in the fall, possibly a new season in our life. I believe not only does God allow the leaves to fall from the trees, but opens the windows of heaven and sends his blessings to His people. Look for His blessings. Remember, we are subject to God's timing, not ours. Amen."

Outside, a section had been cornered off with a string of lights. The sight sparked memories of the hotel courtyard wedding that ignited memories of Dominique's nuptials.

Blake had come to her rescue in Charleston. *I miss him,* she mused.

On Saturday, Paige woke excited that Dominique and Ashton would finally return from their honeymoon. All day, she debated whether she should call or wait for her friend to reach out to her.

In the interim, Paige scrutinized Nyla and Tucker's snapshots of them enjoying breakfast at an upscale eatery posted on social media. She was amazed how much of Blake she saw in Tucker. Both men were handsome, but Blake's ruggedness edged out his cousin. Nyla was also four years older than Tucker, but that didn't faze her cousin at all.

Paige could only hope Tucker was a good guy—sincere—and that he and Nyla would both submit to God's plan of salvation.

When she checked Facebook, Blake's photo was staring back at her under her friend requests. She smiled, and it was as if he smiled back. She had to stop second-guessing her decision not to encourage him. To resist temptation contrary to her decision, Paige signed off Facebook for the rest of the day.

Finally, by late evening, Dominique's familiar ringtone chimed. "Welcome home!" Paige tamed herself from screaming.

"I'm glad to be back." Her friend sounded as if she was gushing. "Paige, the Mediterranean is sooo beautiful. You have to go."

"We were supposed to, remember?" Paige did her best to mask her disappointment and come off as putting a guilt trip on her friend.

"I know," Dominique whined, "but promise me you'll go on your honeymoon, and we can compare notes."

"You do know I have to be married to go on a honeymoon, don't you?"

Dominique giggled. "Silly, your future husband can be around the corner—literally—and you don't know."

"Your husband was supposed to have the hook-up at the wedding, but what did he do? Pick all married groomsmen."

They both chuckled.

"Don't think I didn't do my part. Anyway, if you're not doing anything, come over. Ashton and I are going to open our wedding gifts. I can't believe we got so many. Plus, I brought you back souvenirs from every spot we visited along the Mediterranean Sea like Costa del Sol, Spain. We walked on the beach at the Dead Sea…"

"Wow. Sounds amazing."

"It was, and romantic," Dominique said.

"Aww. All I got you was a T-shirt and snow globe from Charleston." She had visited the gift shop Sunday morning while she waited for Blake.

"You know I love snowglobes. How was the reunion? Anything exciting happen?"

Aside from Blake Cross? "Girl, there were two reunions going on at the same time."

"Can't wait to swap stories. Hurry up and get over here, sister," Dominique said and disconnected.

Paige smiled. Her heart warmed. It was like old times.

Chapter 11

Apparently, Paige was going to play hard to get, and God was going to make it hard for him to get her. For almost a week, he'd heard nothing from her while Tucker had connected with Paige's cousin.

His father's words kept playing in his head.

"Finish what you start, son," Blake Sr. said, referring to Blake quitting Cleveland State University after one semester. "Now, you're about to serve our country. Don't return with a dishonorable discharge. Complete your mission—personal and professional. Make us proud…"

At the time, Blake didn't know his unit would be activated and deployed to Iraq. It was as if his father knew his part-time commitment as a guardsman would turn into a career in the army.

When he separated from active duty, his DD Form 214 document from the United States Department of Defense was evidence that Blake had made his family, especially his father proud. He had accomplished his career mission. Now, he was going after Paige Blake with the same determination to finish what they started in Charleston. Something clicked between them, and it felt right when they were together.

Thanks to his generous tax-free re-enlistment bonuses,

Blake had money in the bank, and he received a small monthly disability check for severe headaches that resulted from a concussion. That money gave him time to breathe and come up with a strategy for the next phase in his life, which he had been indecisive about prior to the reunion. He had options: find a civilian job within the government, return to the classroom, or continue with the military, either through the Reserves or re-enlist with the Ohio National Guardsman where his military career began. Blake needed direction—or as Paige would call it, Godly intervention.

He couldn't say her name or think about her without smiling. She asked if he listened for the Lord to talk back when he prayed. In all honesty, he prayed with little expectation that God would respond. As a soldier, he considered his faith as strong as his comrades, yet Paige brought clarity to the Bible.

Sunday morning, Blake woke with a thirst for some inspiration—new. He recalled the feeling of contentment sharing space with Paige at the church in Charleston. Of course, he could go online and watch streaming services, but it was something about the church atmosphere he had missed being away and wanted to experience again—he wished with her.

On the day of Pentecost, on the day of Pentecost… The wind seemed to carry God's whisper.

What did that mean? He Googled Pentecostal churches. The Day of Pentecost Church jumped out at him as if he had been slapped. His heart did somersaults. Was it this easy for God to direct him?

The church wasn't far from the Richmond Heights home Blake shared for the moment with his parents in the University Circle area. He noted the time of service and got ready. He retrieved his Bible, which had traveled with him all over the world, yet it showed little wear from use.

By the time he walked downstairs, his parents had left for the church he had grown up in and outgrown by the time he deployed.

Taking Monticello Boulevard, he arrived at the church in no time. Surprisingly, the building was a mixture of old and new architecture. He parked in the paved lot across the street. He hiked a dozen steps to an old stone entrance. Once inside, the foyer was newly renovated as far as he could see. The atmosphere was as peaceful and welcoming as it had been last week in Charleston. An usher pointed him to a random pew near the back, and Blake made himself comfortable after resting his Bible on the seat. Stretching out his arms, he glanced around. The sanctuary could easily hold thousands, yet he guessed the members sprinkled throughout amounted to hundreds.

He clapped to the musician's beat and hummed along with the singers. Would Paige consider him off beat again? Blake missed her. How was that possible after one weekend? But it was true. Her absence was felt.

Soon, the congregation settled down as a woman approached the podium and introduced herself as Pastor Katie Wyles. Before her sermon, the pastor's angelic voice bellowed out a song that enticed many to their feet. Lifting their hands in the air, some members had tears streaming down their cheeks unchecked.

Blake sat captivated as he listened to the words, "Here I am to worship…Here I am…" Her voice drifted until a hush spread across the sanctuary. "Amen," she said a couple of times, then opened her Bible. Instantly, the verse appeared on an overhead screen.

"In Matthew six," Pastor Wyles began as some flipped through pages or tapped the app on their tablet or phone, "verse thirty-three says, *But seek ye first the kingdom of God, and His righteousness; and all these things shall be added unto you.* What things?" She stepped back from the podium and scanned the audience as if she was a professor in a lecture hall before returning to the microphone. "Nothing is too small or too great for the Lord to provide us. The key is to desire spiritual knowledge, spiritual wealth, and strive for spiritual discipline."

That struck a chord with him. For fourteen years, Blake was under the command and answered to the whim of the United States Army, and he followed their instructions to the letter. If he chose this type of Christian commitment, the freedom that was just returned to him would be surrendered again to God. What would happen to his freedom?

Come to Me and see My Liberty, God whispered in the midst of the preaching, referring to Second Corinthians 3:17.

Before he could question how, the preacher intercepted, "This chapter is packed with wisdom on how sanctified believers should live, think, and act." She pointed to her Bible. "When your heart is troubled, heavy, or full of sorrow, reread this passage and rest. Trust Jesus to calm the uneasiness…"

For the most part, his basic needs were met. It was Paige he desired. What was the formula to get inside her heart? That was a code worth cracking.

That Sunday evening, after enjoying dinner with his family and easy conversation, Blake retired to his old bedroom. The sermon was still on his mind as he was about to watch a baseball game, but he decided to check Facebook on his phone first. His blood pressure spiked and his adrenaline soared. "Paige accepted my friend request." He noted when and couldn't believe it was last night! Why hadn't he checked before now?

The details didn't matter as he grinned, then pumped his arm in the air and shouted quietly, "Thank You, Jesus!" The Lord indeed answered prayers.

Yet, I still am waiting on you to accept My salvation request. God didn't whisper this time.

Yeah, about that. Blake scratched his head. What did God want from him?

Chapter 12

After leaving Dominique and Ashton's house Saturday night, Paige made a hasty decision. She confirmed Blake's friend request, then second-guessed herself. The longing came after witnessing the newlyweds' love, which was so tangible, Paige could have stuffed a lot of it in her purse and it still would ooze out. Blake's smile flashed before her eyes, but she hadn't mentioned his name to Dominique. She had hoped Blake would have reached out to her by the time she returned home from Sunday's service—nothing. Facebook showed he hadn't logged in for more than sixteen hours. His lack of response triggered memories to escape her mind like animals released into the wild. She couldn't control in which direction they wandered.

To tame her emotions, she pacified herself by perusing Blake's profile. She noted his number of friends. There were plenty of pictures of him posing with other soldiers. Not only did he look fierce in his uniform, Paige dared to say he looked sexy. Blake's smile captured her attention. It was a mixture of sweet and spicy.

She was about to close Facebook when she stumbled across a picture of them sitting in a familiar spot in the hotel lobby. Her breath caught, and she slowly exhaled. Straining her eyes, she clicked to enlarge the photo. They hadn't posed for a picture or taken a selfie, but somehow someone had seized their moment in time.

Judging from what she was wearing, the snapshot was taken Saturday after her hotel wedding breakdown. What had they been discussing? Zooming in on Blake, she scrutinized his expression. Whatever she was saying, his concentration was intense. Although Paige couldn't make out her own expression, she was able to interpret her body language—relaxed.

Why did Blake consume her thoughts after she'd heard a dynamic sermon, "Surrendering to God's Will" from Jeremiah 29:11—*For I know the thoughts that I think toward you, says the Lord, thoughts of peace, and not of evil, to give you an expected end?* We have to trust God until the end of our situations, trials, and blessings," her pastor had said. "In this passage, the devil could only hold God's chosen people for so long. For the Israelites, it was seventy years. I don't believe our trials will last most of our life, if we are faithful to Him…"

After the benediction, Paige had left the church, asking God if she had been faithful in a few things, so He would reward her with many. She reflected on Matthew 25:21: *His lord said unto him, Well done, thou good and faithful servant: thou hast been faithful over a few things, I will make thee ruler over many things: enter thou into the joy of thy Lord.*

By Monday morning while Paige was driving to work, she refused to give Blake any more thought. Soon, Paige parked in the employee lot behind the building that housed Safe Style Designs. After greeting her colleagues, she got situated at her station.

One last time she couldn't resist checking Facebook. Although Blake hadn't reached out, her heart fluttered when she read something inspirational posted on his wall:

Major decisions ahead. Hoping God will help me make the right choice.

Impressed, she liked the comment, pleased he had acknowledged God, then refocused on tasks that needed her attention.

Working as an interior designer for a Fortune 100 company, she had to sketch designs specific to the client's vision and goals in her computer-aided drawing program, or CAD. The sample boards she and her colleagues had presented to Hardcastle Tech Studios had won them a multimillion-dollar contract.

Her company had to keep safety codes and environmental guidelines in the forefront—carpet selection had to be fire resistant, floor tile had to be slip proof. They had to consider easy access to exits, aisles, and corridors, which had to be a certain width and height in their designs for quick evacuations.

It was almost six o'clock when Paige realized many of her coworkers had already left for the day. She was about to try one more layout before going home when her cell phone distracted her. "Hello."

"Are you busy, Miss Blake?"

Her heart skipped. Blake's smooth, deep voice was unforgettable. How did he get her number? She spied her phone and realized he had called her through Facebook Messenger.

"I didn't think you would call me," she said in an accusatory tone.

"I didn't think you wanted me to," he replied honestly, which made her feel like a hypocrite. "You didn't give me your number." When Paige didn't respond, he continued, "I miss you."

Her heart melted at his declaration, but she was afraid to say anything.

"Come on, I'm putting my feelings on the line here. At least talk back to me."

There was no pretense with this guy. "I've missed you too." *There*. She'd professed it.

He laughed. "See, was that so hard?" Did he coo?

She giggled. "No."

"Are you busy?"

"Yep. Still at work." She glanced at the changes she'd made to her design in CAD.

"It's nearly seven. Is anyone else there with you? How long do you plan to stay? How far a drive are you from home?"

Although she was amused that he cared, Paige rolled her eyes. "You're starting to sound like Benjamin."

"Oh no, not the big brother. Seriously, I think I have every right to have an interest in you."

"Why is that?" Lifting a brow, she smirked.

"Because you're carrying my name."

It was something about the way Blake said it that made her suck in her breath. To carry a man's name would mean she had a husband—that's the way he made it sound. That's not what he meant, was it? *Whew*. She shook her head. "By the way, what does the V stand for in your middle name?"

"Vincent."

Blake Vincent Cross, she mouthed silently. He seemed more like a Vance. "Well, I guess you need to let me go so I can finish up these designs and get home before dark, Mr. Cross."

"Letting go isn't as easy as you make it sound." His statement carried another innuendo. "Would it be too much to ask for you to call me when you get home?"

"No," she uttered, before disconnecting.

Blake watched the time, waiting for Paige to call him. Yesterday, it took sheer willpower not to call her back. He coaxed himself into believing the restraint was necessary to show Paige she didn't control all the cards. His emotions caved in, he conceded to defeat and threw in his hand of cards. At exactly nineteen hundred hours and fifteen minutes, she called him back—through Messenger.

He answered with a smile. "If Facebook went down, we would lose all contact."

"Somehow, I think you would find me." She laughed.

She was right. He grabbed his remote and aimed it at his flat screen, one of the few possessions he had purchased since returning home. Maybe he could get her to decorate his place whenever he moved. "I bet you're a great decorator."

"I am, after I design the interiors first."

"Is there a difference?" At full attention, he wanted to mentally document her answers, so he could retrieve them at any time.

"Yep. I have to take exams, which include passing a certification exam to become a licensed designer. Then I have to obtain an apprenticeship to get hands-on experience."

He was impressed. "I'm in awe of you, Miss Blake. You have beauty, spiritual depth..." He paused. Maybe that's what he was lacking, depth with his relationship with God. He refocused, "and intellect, a complete gift-wrapped package." He took a deep breath and showed his true hand. "I was also worried about you."

"What do you mean?"

"When I saw you crying, it tore my heart apart. I was hurting without knowing what and who had hurt you." She was so quiet, Blake doubted she would disclose the source of her pain.

She sighed heavily. "I was having a moment, thinking about my best friend's wedding the week before and how much I missed her, but Dominique and her hubby are back now. I went over to her house and watched them open all their gifts, so I'm good," she rambled.

They talked for hours until he heard her yawn, and they said their good nights. Over the next few days, he and Paige had established a pattern: morning wake-up calls and nightly good night calls, all through Messenger.

One morning, he chuckled when she said, "You do know that I'm already awake when you call me."

"Umm-hmm," Blake teased. He was used to rising early but had slacked off since his army separation. "If that's your story and you're sticking with it, then who am I to contradict the lady who has sleep in her voice when I call."

They chatted about the weather and their hobbies, but she always skirted around any mention that involved them in a relationship. Their conversation never ended without Paige praying for him, followed by a Scripture for meditation. Why couldn't she pray for them instead of him?

"Oh, by the way, here's my number," she stated that same morning before ending their call.

That privilege gave Blake the boost he needed to up his pursuit. After a couple of weeks of talking on the phone, Blake wanted to gaze into those hypnotic eyes and smell her intoxicating perfume, which arrested his senses in the elevator. He was ready to get behind the wheel of his newly purchased SUV for a road trip to St. Louis. The big question was whether she was ready to see him?

While sitting on the patio and enjoying plates piled high, Blake and his father chatted between bites about nothing serious. Blake Sr. asked, "So what's your plan, son?"

That was a question Blake couldn't answer before meeting Paige. Now, he had given himself non-military orders to pursue her. "I'm going to speak with the National Guard recruiter tomorrow."

"You're re-enlisting? You just got home." Lily Cross froze at their table on her way to the grill.

"As a reservist, Mom." Blake didn't want his mother working herself into a frenzy like she had years ago when he was deployed.

"Oh." She relaxed. "I thought since you've been visiting that church, you were settling in here. I mean there's no rush for you to find a place."

Soon his sisters appeared at their mother's side. "Maybe it's time to tie the knot," Monique said. "If you need pretty prospects, say the word and I'm on it."

He withheld his smirk. If they wanted to see a pretty woman, Monique and Sanette should have seen Paige. Folding his arms, Blake looked over his shoulder at his other sister. Although they were closer in age, she was just as bossy as Monique. "Haven't heard from you."

Sanette shrugged. "I'm just glad to have my baby brother back home."

Memories of feeling smothered by the women in his family resurfaced. His sisters were overly protective when he was a boy, even as a teenager. Fourteen years ago, at the age of twenty, he and his father discussed the military as being his best option for independence. It was time to stretch his wings again.

Chapter 13

"You're where?" Paige's mind flashed "Warning" before her eyes as she sat behind the wheel at a stoplight. In contrast, her heart fluttered like an excited butterfly at the news.

Although it had been almost a month since she'd smelled Blake's cologne, suddenly the fragrance tickled her nose as if he was sitting in the passenger seat.

Blake's chuckle was low. "In St. Louis, Miss Blake.

"Ah, since when?" Paige couldn't stop herself from peeping at her appearance in the rearview mirror as she headed home. After working forty-plus hours this week, she looked every bit like she had earned her salary.

"An hour ago. I thought I'd surprise you."

"Oh, you did."

"I'm hoping you will let me take you out to dinner."

She didn't know how she felt about surprises at the moment. "Umm-hmm. Why?"

"Number one, because I'm serving my country this weekend as a reservist."

Paige blinked, still dumbfounded that Blake was in her city. "Here?" she repeated.

"I can serve anywhere in the country, so why not here? The number two, three, four, and more reasons are to see you once a month."

His admission frightened and excited her until Paige

wasn't sure which had dominance. She hadn't realized she was smiling until she turned her head and briefly made eye contact with the male driver in the next car. He returned a smile of his own.

"I thought you ended your military career."

"Active duty, yes, but the military will always be a part of me. I have to report in the morning at zero seven hundred hours. Tonight is open, so will you let me take you to dinner?"

His request was a bit tempting, but if he wanted her, he would have to take the bait. "How about you join me for the singles ministry at my church? We have snacks afterward, but nothing hearty."

"I'll be there." He didn't hesitate as he took the church's name, address, and the time of service. "See you at seven-thirty."

Paige blinked. *He took the bait. Lord, is this part of Your will for me, or Blake?* The unknown caused her to shiver. Due to a stalled car that backed up rush-hour traffic, Paige finally made it home and had exactly one hour to shower, change, and make herself presentable.

Despite her reservations, Paige was excited about seeing Blake again. When he first called her, she didn't expect to talk to him every day, it just happened. Now, it was routine to hear his deep voice. Funny, Blake hadn't mentioned he was en route to St. Louis that morning.

If only Dominique and Ashton hadn't taken another three-hour weekend getaway to the Lake of the Ozarks, they could meet Blake. The newlyweds had stayed weeks earlier at the same resort for the Labor Day weekend. This time the couple was traveling with two other church couples for an impromptu retreat.

She sighed as she stepped into the shower. She missed her bond with Dominique and the ability to share every high and low point in their lives, anytime, day or night. Blake being in town was one of those high points. She hadn't been this excited to see a man in a long time, not even when Brother Kenneth Warner invited her to a gospel concert. Paige learned later that she'd "won" the date with him after three other sisters had turned him down. Clearly, they knew something she didn't—Brother Warner wasn't looking for marriage, only a good time.

After rinsing off, Paige got out of the shower. Taking a towel, she cleared the condensation on the mirror and looked at her reflection. Her hair was in the in-between hair appointment stage. The best she could do was to brush it into a ball on top of her head before she applied her makeup. With Dominique out of pocket, she called Claire.

"Hey, cuz," she answered cheerfully.

"Hey back. I need prayer, advice, and more prayer," Paige said on speakerphone.

Claire gasped. "What's wrong? Aunt Miranda okay? Uncle Will? Your brothers—" Paige chuckled and assured her everyone was fine. "Whew, you almost gave me a heart attack."

"Sorry." Paige dabbed concealer under her eyes. "My heart needs prayers. Blake's in town. He says he's here for army drills, or whatever you call it, *and* to see me."

"Hmm. That's an impressive agenda."

"I know." She paused to clean up a lipstick smear on the counter. "I invited him to church tonight, and he accepted with little coaxing."

"Amen."

"It would help if I could tap into where he is in his

salvation walk with the Lord. I can't let myself get serious without knowing he has strong ties with Jesus." Paige huffed before applying a few strokes of mascara on her lashes. "I definitely didn't try to encourage him."

"You didn't have to. I'm sure you were sending out disinterested-in-a-relationship vibes, but they bounced off as if his body was a shield." Claire added, "Plus, I caught him watching you when you weren't thinking about him— or maybe you were. Anyway, trust me, you enthralled him without trying. The mothers at my church have a saying, 'a woman makes the best fisherman of men. If a man wants a woman, he will go into the water to be caught. I think Blake is watching for the hook to latch onto. As a matter of fact, maybe he's on his Damascus Road."

Paige considered her cousin's assessment. "If only it was that easy to get a husband, but he's got to go deep into the Word for me. I don't like fishing anyway. Besides, a woman shouldn't be the one to cast out a hook. I've guarded my heart for years. Somehow, Blake has touched my senses, so please pray for me—and him." Closing her eyes, she bowed her head and waited for Claire to begin.

"Father, in the mighty name of Jesus—" Paige shivered at the power associated with the Lord's name— "You are magnificent in all Your ways. You said if we acknowledge You, You will direct our paths. Please bless my cousin with a man who will love You and her. Let Blake know that the way to my cousin's heart is through You. Give Paige wisdom, and let her fall in love because I like Blake. In Jesus' name. Amen," she rushed to finish, then giggled.

Paige blinked in surprise. "Couldn't stay unbiased, huh?"

"Nope. Bye."

After eating dinner alone at the hotel restaurant, Blake set off to see Paige against the backdrop of her church. He entered the address for Salvation Temple in his GPS and headed in that direction. Minutes from his destination, Blake made a detour to a small floral shop he almost passed. Seconds inside the store, a floral arrangement grabbed Blake's attention. The red, yellow, and purple petals reminded him of Paige's personality.

Without knowing it, she had set some things in motion. His parents, sisters, and even the recruiter questioned his judgment to join the reserves out of state. The idea had struck him odd too, but by the time he made it to the recruiter's office, his mind was made up. Blake felt like a puppy on a leash, and it wasn't all Paige's doing. He had told them the truth. "My future is there."

"St. Louis!" his mother had practically shrieked. "Why would you re-enlist to travel outside the state for your monthly drill instead of at one closer to home?" The frustration was apparent. "You'll be paying the government for a service they're supposed to pay you for."

Everyone's arguments were valid. To a civilian or veteran, his thinking might not make sense, but his heart was one hundred percent on board with it. "Like that old song, 'Meet Me in St. Louis,' I feel God is drawing me there, Mom. Plus, Paige lives there, and I want to finish what we started at the reunion."

"The beautiful woman you were talking to instead of being at your own family reunion banquet."

Blake shook his head. "Mom, don't make it sound like a conspiracy. I left to get my wallet from the room. I saw her...and we talked. We have some things in common and we enjoyed each other's company."

His sister had lifted a suspicious eyebrow. "How come I didn't meet her?" Monique shot him an accusatory glare.

That had started a round of twenty questions about Paige, and he was only able to answer half of them. He reached across the table and took his mother's hand. "I have to see if she is the one. You want grandbabies, right?"

The light returned to her eyes as she perked up. "I'll help you pack."

Blake pulled his mind back to the present. Paige's requirement for a brotha wasn't the standard athletic build, which he had, looks, and money. She wanted a super spiritual man, and he was weak in that area. And she had called him out for not reading his Bible.

His heart rate accelerated as he spied the church's sign, noting the meticulous care given to the plush lawn. The entrance was welcoming as he turned into Salvation Temple's lot. Suddenly, his confidence slipped. Would Paige be as glad to see him as he was to see her?

Once he parked, he got out and glanced around, recalling the day he'd visited Day of Pentecost Church and wishing she had been there. With flowers in hand, he took long strides to the entrance, his heart pounding with every step.

A tall man, about the same age and height as Blake was in the hallway giving instructions to someone on the phone. Looking up, he smiled, then mouthed, "Praise the Lord."

"Can you tell me where the singles ministry is being held?" Blake tried to mouth back.

He pointed to the left, and Blake followed the sounds of voices. Trained to be fearless, Blake fought back a bout of anxiety as he was about to come face-to-face with the woman he wanted more than anything at the moment.

When he stood in the doorway, the buzz of

conversations ceased. Nodding, he moved farther into the room and scanned the faces until he located his target. When Paige made eye contact with him, her smile brightened the room. He exhaled.

She stood and waved him to where she was sitting. "Hi." Her hazel eyes captivated him.

"Do I at least get a hug?" He handed her the flowers.

Blushing, she accepted his offering and squeezed him so quickly that he didn't have time to trap her in a satisfying embrace.

Once she sat, he did too, but he couldn't keep from staring. "You're more beautiful than I remember." She continued to blush.

"I've been attending church in Cleveland." Her eyes lit up at his admission. "It doesn't feel the same without you there."

"Awww, thank you, but the main attraction is Jesus. You don't need me."

He reached for her hand and squeezed it. "Yes, I do."

"Praise the Lord, everyone," said the same man who was in the hall.

Paige slipped her hand out of his. "That's Minister Quinton Ray, our singles leader."

"I see a few new faces tonight. I won't put you on the spot, but welcome." Minister Ray nodded at Blake.

"Am I the only guest here?" he asked.

"Oh, no," Paige assured him. "We have new visitors every week." She craned her neck and looked around. "There's at least a dozen I don't recognize."

Blake relaxed as Paige sniffed the flowers. He smiled as she closed her eyes. That's when he noticed how long her lashes were.

"Tonight, my wife, Sister Mya, and I thought it would be fun to play a couple of rounds of the Dating Game, and we're looking for volunteers. Three brothers."

"Should I raise my hand," Blake teased, scooting closer to Paige.

"No, silly." She slapped his hand. "Just watch, listen, and learn," she whispered.

Once the three contestants were settled in chairs, facing the crowd of less than a hundred, Sister Mya began the game. "We know from the Bible that man was God's greatest creation and love. He was concerned about Adam before Adam realized he was alone. God created a perfect mate for him. I emphasize 'perfect' for him."

Right away, the woman had Blake's attention.

"There's a reason why the man is the head of the woman, and God is the head of a man. When there was trouble in paradise, Adam didn't take the lead. Let's start off our first set of questions with our bachelors to see how they would take the lead in certain situations."

Some women chuckled, others clapped, and the men seemed embarrassed.

"Bachelor number one, when it comes to relationships, what is your definition of protection—and we're not talking about sex paraphernalia?"

Blake withheld his smirk, even though the question was amusing.

"As a man of God, my job is to protect a sister's soul when we're on a date at all costs. If I love her, then I'm to protect her heart from being hurt and take the punches."

Deep, Blake thought. He definitely wouldn't have given that answer.

Sister Mya turned to the second contestant. "Bachelor

number two, a very pretty woman makes it known she likes you, but she doesn't attend church, read her Bible, or seem interested in worshiping God. You're attracted to her. What do you do?"

Blake folded his arms. Yeah, what was a brother supposed to do with that one?

"Whew." Bachelor number two exhaled. The room was still. "Pray," he said as some chuckled. "I mean, if we're attracted to each other, I would have to pray and try to draw her to Christ. If she's not interested after a few attempts, I'll pray even harder that God would give me the strength to cut my losses."

"That seems so severe," Blake mumbled to Paige.

Shaking her head, she stared at him. "Hell is hot. There's a reason why God warns us against temptations."

They played two rounds, and Blake found the answers to be thought-provoking.

"Let's give our brothers a hand for their honest answers. Now, I need three sister volunteers," Minister Ray said, taking the mic from his wife.

When Paige motioned to stand, Blake gently restrained her. "If you want me to know something, tell me in private."

"Okay." She giggled. "Just making sure you're alert."

"Very." He stared into her eyes and held it until she looked away.

Clearing her throat, she smiled. "I'm glad you came and could see how serious we are about our Christian conduct and salvation."

Before he could say more, Minister Ray chose the three contestants and commanded Paige's attention.

"Sisters, I'm going to stay in the Book of Genesis. When God told Adam not to eat of the fruit from the Tree of Life,

Eve hadn't been created. The Bible doesn't tell us if Adam passed that message down to Eve or not. We do know Eve was beguiled by a smooth talker. Satan is known for spewing half-truths." He glanced at his index cards. "Contestant number one, if you meet a guy who seems nice, is that enough for you to trust him?"

The woman gnawed on her lips. "For me," she started, "I would trust him until he shows me another side." She twisted her lips as if she was second-guessing herself. "Somehow, I feel that's not the right answer."

"Remember, sisters, our natural eyes can miss things," Minister Ray said. "I would suggest you pray and let the Holy Ghost search all things, including that person's soul, like in First Corinthians 2:10."

Blake nudged Paige, and she playfully nudged him back. "I see now why you're so hard on a brother."

Although Blake teased Paige, he noted the women's answers seemed heartfelt, and he appreciated their raw honesty.

Minister Ray ended the game after two rounds. "In conclusion, you all are winners because you know the Word of God. Use it."

Everyone applauded, even Blake, then he turned to Paige. "Please don't use the Bible against me. I'm trying here."

"God knows. Plus, Second Timothy 3:16 says, '*All scripture is given by inspiration of God, and is profitable for doctrine, for reproof, for correction, for instruction in righteousness.*' So don't be scared."

Blake wasn't scared-per se, but wondered if he would have the right answers for Paige to take him seriously.

Chapter 14

Paige didn't realize she was dreaming until a ringtone annoyed her. Grasping for her phone on the nightstand, she answered. "Hello?"

"I can't believe you're still sleeping while I waited up most of the night to hear what happened," Claire fussed.

"What time is it?" Paige still hadn't opened her eyes.

"It's eight o'clock."

"Eight on Saturday morning?" She rolled on her back. "No wonder I'm still asleep."

"Oh, no you don't. Wake up. You asked me to pray, so now I want to hear about the fruits of my labor. So how is Blake?"

"Handsome as ever. Sweet." Paige forced her lashes to flutter until they opened. Her bedroom came into focus, and so did the memories of last night. "Our singles ministry played rounds of the Dating Game. It was perfect. The timing couldn't have been better for him to hear what it takes to be in a godly relationship. Afterward, a couple of us went out to eat. Although I wasn't ready for our night to end, he had drills this morning, so we said good night."

"That's it? No romantic vibes?" Claire sighed.

"There is nothing sexier than a man who hungers and thirsts after God's righteousness. He was genuinely interested in the Dating Game's Q&A. Blake walked me to my car. The moment was surreal as we stared into each other's eyes, wondering what the other was thinking. I could tell he was battling to say something—or maybe to kiss me." She pouted. "Instead, he wrapped me in his arms and seemed reluctant to release me. He told me to text him when I made it home, and I did."

Their brief embrace spoke to her heart of his tenderness. She wondered what her heart revealed to him. God told her to guard her heart, then to open it. Was it because Blake Cross could eventually be the one? Paige must have drifted off when she heard Claire call her name, then said goodbye. Perfect. She snuggled back under the covers.

Later Saturday afternoon, Paige drove to Olivette to visit with her parents. While her dad was stretched out in his recliner watching a Cardinals baseball game, she and her mother lounged outside on the deck and enjoyed the serenity.

"Do you remember Blake from the family reunion in Charleston?" she asked casually as they sipped on lemonade.

"Yes. The one who had a crush on you," her mother gushed.

Paige giggled. "Yeah, and my crush is here in St. Louis. He came to the singles ministry last night."

Straightening up, her mother's mouth opened, but she seemed too flustered to say anything. She set her glass on the table and gave Paige her full attention. "I thought you didn't plan to stay in contact with him."

"I didn't, but Mr. Cross had other plans. He got in contact with me, and we've been talking ever since. He's here for some military drills this weekend." She couldn't contain her smile. "There's something about Blake that I can't ignore."

"Ignore him," her father said from the doorway. Clearly, he had been eavesdropping. "He's too cocky for me." He grunted.

"That's confidence, Daddy. Blake is a veteran."

"Oh hush, William." Her mother shooed him away, but her father wasn't budging from his spot. "Let's get to know him for Paige's sake, honey." Miranda eyed her husband, then faced Paige again. "Is he coming to church tomorrow?"

"No." Paige shook her head. "Then invite him to dinner tomorrow," Her mother suggested.

"I'll ask him." When her father returned to the game, Paige lowered her voice. "Mom, I'm scared."

"I knew it," her father roared and reappeared. "What has he done?"

Paige sighed and stood. "Nothing, Daddy. Can't I have a mother-daughter talk in private? We'll talk later, Mom. I'm heading home."

Miranda got to her feet and forced her fists to her hips. "You see what you did? You're scaring Paige away." She pointed to a patio chair. "Stay, sweetie. Goodbye, William Blake."

Paige complied as they both waited for her father to disappear into the house. Huddling close together, her mother told her to proceed. "Now, what's going on?"

"I like him. He's caring, funny, and..."

"Handsome," her mother filled in.

Paige shook her head. "I believe he wants a stronger walk with God, but I'm not sure."

Her mother wrapped her arm around Paige's shoulder

and squeezed her closer. "Be strong enough for the both of you, and pray until God draws him." Nodding, Paige smiled before her mother continued, "Or until your next birthday, then move on."

Laughing together, the two exchanged a high five. "Sounds like a plan." This time when she stood, Paige did say her goodbyes.

She had hoped Blake would call her after he finished his drills. By six o'clock when she still hadn't heard from him, she called to invite him to her parents' house for dinner.

"Hello." He sounded as if he was under heavy drugs.

"Are you asleep?"

"Taking a nap. Sorry, babe. The drill wiped me. I was going to call you when I woke up."

His endearment didn't escape her. Did he even realize he'd said it? She smiled. "Get your rest. My parents would like to invite you to dinner tomorrow."

He was quiet. "I had planned to drive back to Cleveland."

"A night driver."

"It's the best time to think, but I wouldn't miss the chance to spend more time with you. Count me in." He yawned.

"Good night." No doubt last night's activities had probably added to his fatigue. Before going to bed, she prayed, *Lord, Blake's here for military obligations. How do I fit into all this?*

God didn't answer.

The next day, after completing his drills, Blake followed

his GPS directions to Paige's parents' house. He admired the quiet neighborhood as he turned on the street. Judging from the cars in the driveway and in front of the ranch home, he wasn't the only guest as he had assumed.

He parked, and the front door opened as he got out of the car. Paige stood in the doorway. The hem of her bright sundress against her tanned brown skin swayed in the gentle wind.

He discreetly admired her legs and the dark polish on her toenails. Blue had to be her favorite color. It was the same shade she wore the night of her family's banquet. Although he would have liked to see her hair around her shoulders, she had brushed it up into a ball again.

"Wow."

"Hi, honey. Welcome home," Paige barely said with a straight face.

He smirked as he measured each step that would lead him to the porch. He didn't stop until he towered over her and removed his cap. He grinned—or maybe he was blushing. Either way, happiness filled his being. He inched closer to her lips, coaxing her to meet him halfway. She didn't move. He lifted a brow. "Hi, dear—or should I say princess? Do I get a welcome home kiss and hug?"

She giggled, tilting her head, then she did blush. Stabbing her long finger in his chest, she pushed him back—or tried. He didn't budge this time. "Sorry. I don't think that's a good idea, but I couldn't resist saying that. You look so cute in your uniform."

The uniform had that effect every time on a woman. "You've never noticed a man in a uniform before?"

"They've never been you."

He swallowed. Her words were powerful. The door

opened wider before he had a comeback. Her brother, Benjamin, stood behind her. To Blake's surprise, he gave him a salute. It was comical, but Blake returned it.

"Only because you're in uniform. Come on in."

"At ease, Ben." Paige rolled her eyes, then fumbled for Blake's hand.

He allowed her to lead him inside. Familiar faces from the reunion greeted him, and a few more. There had to be a dozen people. After the introductions were made, he was shown to the bathroom where he could wash his hands.

At the table, Blake's stomach growled with anticipation as he readied himself for a feast. Instead, he found himself in the hot seat—evidently, a prerequisite for his meal.

Those who identified themselves as neighbors wanted to know about his military career. Paige's sisters-in-law, Faith and Gina, were interested in the sights and sounds of Cleveland. They seemed friendly and no threat, then it got personal.

"Having big brothers has its benefits." Raymond winked at Paige who squinted back. "Warning, you haven't seen a war like the one we will start if you hurt her." His nostrils flared like an attack dog.

"Ray!" Paige's voice thundered.

Blake took her hand and squeezed it. "I'm good. I'm a baby brother, so I know all about the fury of older siblings, especially women. My duty is to protect, serve, and defend our country against conflicts. My mentality hasn't changed when it comes to Paige."

That earned him a squeeze, plus a look of awe glowing from every woman's face.

Mr. Cross cleared his voice. A hush fell on the room instantly. "Blake, are you married, separated, or divorced?"

"No, sir." Blake kept eye contact with her father, although he felt Paige stiffen.

"Do you have any children that you claim or don't claim?" He gave Blake a deadpan expression, indicating that no subject was off the table. Again, Blake answered, "No, sir." If they didn't feed him soon, he would get a plate to go. Folding his arms, Paige's father leaned back in the chair. "So what are your intentions concerning my daughter?"

Facing Paige, Blake was immediately drawn into her hazel eyes. He blinked before she lured him into a trance. "We're trying to figure that out." She smiled.

"Once you do, I want to be the first to know." Mr. Cross patted his hand on the table. "Okay, let's eat."

When Blake readied himself to leave, Paige pulled him to the side and apologized for her family's interrogation. "I might be the baby brother, but my threats were just as real when it came to my sisters. No man was going to mess with them. I might not have been tall or all muscle back then—" he demonstrated by flexing his biceps—"but I knew people who knew people."

She laughed and guided him to the door, and they both stepped out to the porch. Blake adjusted his cap on his head. She closed the door behind her, then squeezed him tight. When Paige lingered in his arms, he realized she was praying. "Father, in the powerful name of Jesus, please guide Blake home safely and send Your angels to protect him and other travelers on the road, by water, rail, or air. Lord, perform Your perfect will in his life. In Jesus' name. Amen."

"Amen." He brushed a kiss on top of her head as she hastily stepped back.

His soul seemed always to be on her mind. Touched, he

stroked her cheek with the back of his hand, knowing his palm was coarse from this weekend's workout. "Thank you for that."

"Any time, and all the time. Call me when you get home."

Frowning, Blake shook his head. "No. It'll be too late, and you have to work in the morning. Call me when you wake up."

"I guess I'll be waking up in eight hours." She grinned. "Good night." Spinning around, Paige walked back into the house, leaving him to crave a good night or goodbye kiss until next time.

Chapter 15

Paige tracked Blake's taillights until they disappeared, then Dominique's ringtone brought her out of the trance.

"Hey, girl. We're back home. What are you doing?"

"Watching Blake drive off. Your timing is terrible. I wish you'd met him."

"Who's Blake? I can't remember any of your cousins going by his last name."

If only her friend could see Paige blush. "It's a long story, but Blake likes me—"

"What? Hold it right there. I'm coming to your place tomorrow after work. You went and got yourself a boyfriend on me...uh-huh." Paige imagined Dominique shaking her head and wagging her finger. "I'd be over there tonight if you lived next door—or if I wasn't so tired. I drove back while Ashton snored from the passenger seat."

"Hey, I did not," Ashton defended in the background.

"Do you really think the man who has flowers waiting at your office every week is going to let you out of his sight?"

"Depending on his delivery load, he might get home late. Besides, Ash will give me a pass for a few hours." Dominique giggled while Paige gathered her purse and keys.

"And not a minute more. I'm heading out. I'm at Mom and Dad's house."

"Tell them hi." Dominique raised her voice as Paige's parents were nearby and could hear. "Tomorrow is our time. We're long overdue."

"Can't blame it on me. I don't have a tall, medium chocolate, and handsome hunk to come home to every night."

"Humph. Not yet. I'll see if Blake passes the Dominique—" she cleared her throat—"Taylor test."

Paige chuckled at Dominique's use of her new last name. It was so good to hear her friend's voice. "Okay, tomorrow. Bye."

"Bye. Love you, sister," Dominique added.

"Love you too."

She hugged her family goodbye. Dominique's call had spared Paige from giving her brother a piece of her mind.

Back at her apartment, Paige hurried to get her clothes and other things ready for work the next morning in case the wake-up call to Blake might cause her to oversleep afterward.

While doing her task, she smiled and hummed the song the choir sang at service. She enjoyed watching Blake at the singles event and didn't mind him knowing it. She chuckled at his response to Ray's threat—to protect and serve the country and her. That sent shivers down her arms. She wondered if his answer factored in what he'd heard Friday night during the Dating Game.

Before crawling into bed, Paige prayed longer, crying out to Jesus for direction in her life. After saying, "In Jesus' name. Amen," she set her alarm for three a.m., the estimated time Blake should arrive in Cleveland. It seemed like seconds after snuggling under her cover, the alarm jolted her out of her peaceful slumber.

111

She spied the time and groaned. It took a few minutes to figure out why it went off earlier than normal: Blake. Sitting up in her bed, Paige grabbed her phone and tapped his name. He answered right away. "Hey. Are you home yet?"

"Yep. Been here about thirty-eight minutes." He sounded tired. "I really didn't expect you to call, but I'm glad you did."

Why did this man say all the right things to make her heart flutter? His voice was so deep, it could lull her to sleep. "Me too. Good night."

"Paige," he yelled as her finger hovered over the end button. "Thank you."

"For what?"

"For being the one and only Paige Blake. Now, you get some rest."

"Okay," she whispered and reset her alarm. Scooting back into a comfortable position, she closed her eyes. The alarm blared again, too soon. Despite the disruption in her sleep, Paige floated into work that morning, a contrast to how she'd left on Friday. That was before she knew Blake was in town.

Had God sent Blake to add happiness to her life? She couldn't wait to tell Dominique about her Blake namesake.

Most of her morning, she was busy, consulting with engineers and architects out in the field. When she returned to the office, Paige focused on her tasks, so she could be the first one out the door at four-thirty. She stopped at Popeye's for chicken wings and red beans and rice—her and Dominique's favorite—then drove home to make a salad.

Paige's doorbell rang minutes after she kicked off her shoes. She opened the door and screamed her delight at seeing her best friend. After tight hugs, they smacked each other on the cheeks with kisses. Stepping out of their embrace, Dominique walked inside, dropped her purse on a chair, and headed straight to the kitchen sink to wash her hands. "So, from the beginning, I want details," she said, opening Paige's refrigerator and pulling out romaine lettuce and other fixings for the salad as if she was preparing the meal. "I'm listening."

Paige chuckled. "Some things never change," she said, referring to how her friend took charge of the kitchen. It didn't matter where.

"Old habits." Dominique shrugged. Her friend loved to cook, and Paige loved to sample. "But evidently some things have changed. Why am I just now hearing about Blake?"

"Maybe because you're married now and I'm not." Paige spoke her mind without thinking how it sounded. Because of her delivery, their jovial mood dissipated. "Sorry." She twisted her lips, then washed her hands before reaching inside the Popeye's bag for the carryout. "I meant I know my place in your life now. I've stepped back so Ashton can be your best friend." Those words pained her, and she sniffed.

"Hey." Dominique stopped what she was doing and dragged Paige to the sofa. "Ashton will always be the love of my life, but you are my sister. Plus, without you cheering me and Ashton on, I might not be Mrs. Taylor." Her eyes watered.

They had been friends since high school and knew each other too well. "Yeah, you were going to miss your blessing on that one, because it took you a while to see blue collar men rock."

"True." Her friend nodded. "I'm sorry if you think I've

pushed you away. I didn't mean to. If you call me at two in the morning, I'm here." She patted her chest.

"Ashton would probably tag along too."

"Yep." Dominique bobbed her head. "And drive the company vehicle."

Laughing, they worked side by side to make the salad. God reminded Paige that her relationship with Dominique hadn't cracked, but remained as strong as ever.

Once their plates were filled, Paige said grace, then began to give Dominique a day-by-day account of what happened between her and Blake up until the phone call she made that morning. Her friend didn't interrupt as she ate with gusto. Their salads were the first to be devoured.

"Wow. And you thought you were going to have a boring summer. Blake arrived late on the scene. Hmmm, a late summer love." Dominique's eyes sparkled with mischief. "And I thought marrying my deliveryman was a chance meeting, but riding the elevator…"

Once they cleaned the chicken bones and finished off their red beans and rice, Dominique recovered first and slapped the table. "Where's your phone?"

Paige frowned. "In my purse. Why? Did you hear it ring?"

"Nope. Hand it to me," she said adamantly.

Getting to her feet, Paige padded across the kitchen floor, rummaged through her purse, and retrieved her phone. Dominique was reaching for it before Paige could slide it in front of her. "What are you doing?" she asked, watching her friend tap in Paige's password.

"FaceTiming Mr. Cross, of course." Dominique grinned mischievously.

"Are you crazy?" Paige reached for the phone. Too late,

Blake's face filled the screen.

"Hello," he answered, then paused when he realized it wasn't her. "And you are?"

Dominique burst out laughing and nodded. "Yeah, I like him," she told Paige. "Hi, Blake. I'm Dominique, Paige's best friend, and I had to check you out for myself. You sound interesting, maybe even promising, but you'd better get your act together with God first."

Paige snatched her phone back. "You're dismissed." She gritted her teeth at her friend. "Go home to your hubby."

"O-okay. Humph." Dominique stood and began to clear the table. It's what they did—never leave each other's place without straightening it up after eating.

"Sorry about that." She shook her head, eyeing Dominique who was pretending she was disinterested. "I told you we're like sisters, but I'm older."

Dominique spun around, water dripping from her soapy hands. "By one month and a few hours."

"That's twelve hours, and you know it," Paige corrected. Their banter felt good. She and Dominique hadn't had any sister time in a long while.

"It's okay."

Paige felt Dominique looking over her shoulder before she turned around to verify it. Her friend wasn't going to give her any privacy. "That's it. Go home." She gathered Dominique's things and playfully shoved her toward the door. "Do I have to call Ashton on you?" Paige smirked.

"Nope. He's calling me now." Dominique tapped her Bluetooth and pulled her keys from her purse. "Hi, honey." She kissed Paige's cheek, then yelled. "Bye, Blake."

Paige's interaction with her friend amused Blake. He smiled, knowing she was happy, especially after he learned the memories of her friend's wedding were the reason behind Paige's tears.

"Let me call you back. My dad's on the other end."

"Sure." Blake was confident she would call him after speaking with her father. Drumming his fingers on the patio table, he counted down from ten, nine, eight, seven… His phone rang before he got to three, but it wasn't FaceTime. "Hello," he answered in a singsong manner.

"You sent me flowers."

"I did." He nodded. "I would have sent them to you directly, but I only had your parents' address. I hope Mr. Cross didn't think they were for him."

She laughed. "No, silly. Thank you."

Leaning forward, he anchored his elbow on the table and glanced around the yard at the array of fall colors the trees were displaying. It was so easy to be free with his thoughts with her. "You inspire me, Paige. I want you to know that."

"In a good way or godly way?" she asked.

He frowned, surprised by her question. He gave it some thought. "Both, I guess. My relationship with God was never a priority until I met you and saw how personal you take it. You, Paige, are showing me what I've been missing."

"I guess we've both been missing something," she said in a cryptic message she wouldn't explain, even though they were on the phone for almost an hour.

Yes, Paige definitely inspired him, and Blake had told the senior Blake that after he woke from his long drive. *His father had walked through the door at the same time Blake was about*

116

to begin his daily run. *"You're up. How was your trip? Did you see Paige?"*

"Yes. She's as beautiful as ever. I'm leaning toward relocating to St. Louis." He counted to three and waited for his announcement to register.

"You're what? I suggest you lean back this way, son." His father raised his voice, confusion plaguing his face. *"You're making a major life decision based on your attraction to a woman?"* He pounded the counter with his fist. *"I know you suffered a concussion in the Middle East, but I thought you had fully recovered. Evidently not, if you're thinking this irrationally."*

"That's a low blow, Dad." That stung.

He mumbled an apology without meeting Blake's eyes.

Blake loved Cleveland. There was no place like home. Although the weekend drill in St. Louis had been his covert mission to run into battle to win Paige's heart, but God had issued an edict while he was asleep last Thursday night.

She's a woman after My heart, God whispered, then thundered, *You have to come through Me.*

When he got on the road Friday morning, Blake didn't know what was in store for him. Once in St. Louis, he had seen a bigger picture in his life. That Dating Game had done something to him. He thought serving his country made him a man, but serving God gave him a greater purpose. Paige's church ministry had given him a glimpse at what it meant to have a spiritual mindset. *"I said Paige is one of the reasons."*

"The other?" His father twisted his mouth and gave Blake a pointed stare.

"It's hard to explain—"

"Try me." Blake Sr. grunted. *"Clearly, this woman's got in your head bad, and you're willing to go chase after her. When did things get this serious?"* His questions were endless.

117

"It's not all about Paige. I feel God is drawing me there, and somehow my life will change spiritually."

His father huffed. *"Cleveland has a lot of churches."*

"It's not set in stone, but——"

"Good," Blake Sr. said. *"You can chisel out this misjudgment."*

Blake was no longer in the military where he had to take orders, even from his father. *"I'm my own man, Dad. This is my decision to make,"* Blake said with finality, reminding his father he was no longer a little boy who needed direction. They held each other's stare until Blake recognized his father's look—Blake Sr. was hot. His father was not one to be challenged in his house.

Good thing Blake planned to move out and move on. It seemed like God was behind the wheel on this mission, and taking Blake along for the ride.

Although Paige didn't know what he was contemplating, the news spread among his family about this possible move. It didn't make sense to him either, at times, but the urge was strong, and he couldn't ignore it. One by one, his mother, sisters, and aunts tried to talk him out of it, then it seemed as if they put their faith in Tucker to succeed where they couldn't.

"You sure I can't talk you out of doing this, man?" Tucker asked. *"You know I made a snap judgment to fly into Raleigh for breakfast with Nyla. It was nice between us for a little while, but that's over— do not resuscitate. You're talking about more than an overnight bag. What if you two don't work out, then what?"*

Then I hope God has a Plan B for me, he thought. *"Things will work out,"* he said, ending the call, thinking either with Paige or God. Blake wanted both.

Chapter 16

While on her lunch break, Paige was catching up with Dominique and munching on a carrot.

"Will you stop that?" her friend demanded. "I don't think my husband will appreciate me going deaf so early in our marriage."

"Ashton will simply buy you the top-of-the-line hearing aid."

"Yeah." Dominique giggled. "I've got a good man—practicing Christian, godly, Bible reader, doer of the Word, and more. I can never thank Jesus enough for His blessings."

"I want to be able to say those things."

"Maybe you will with Blake. He seems like a sweetheart and didn't fight you on going to church—that's a start. He won me over sending flowers to your dad."

"You know those were meant for me, right?" Shaking her head, Paige crunched on another carrot for the fun of it after dipping it in ranch dressing.

"Ouch, girl," Dominique fussed.

"I really like him," Paige whined. "But I can't compromise."

"Is he asking you to?"

Paige shook her head as if her friend could see her. When

she didn't answer, Dominique asked again. "No."

"Everything will work out according to God's will." Dominique paused. "I'll shuffle him from fifteenth place on my prayer list to number four. He's now in high-priority position."

Paige chuckled. "Who's in the top three spots?"

"Ashton, my marriage, and my love for my husband."

"Should have known. Jesus, I want what she has!" Paige pleaded.

"And God will give you the desires of your heart. Keep delighting yourself in Him."

"Amen. Psalm 37:4. Coming once a month for his training or whatever is probably a good thing. Still, I have to keep reminding myself the man has to completely surrender to God, or we can't have a relationship."

"Umm-hmm."

"If I don't keep saying it, I'll want to experience those soft kisses, strong hugs… Let me stop there. I'm not a married woman and shouldn't entertain those thoughts." She fanned herself, then checked the time. "Lunch is over. Back to my station."

Later when she arrived home, she picked up a small package outside her door. Unwrapping it, there was a Post-it note from Dominique. What was her friend up to now?

It's your turn now, sister. You gave me a copy of God's Love is Perfect for the Single_Sister. *It's time for you to reflect on the passages.*

Inside her apartment, Paige kicked off her heels, dumped her purse on the counter, then padded across the hardwood floors to the large bay window that overlooked Forest Park. After reclining, she opened the journal.

God created Adam and Eve and two of every animal. He knows your loneliness like others can't understand.

Pray hard, believe, and fall in love with Jesus. Worship Him until He gives you a dance partner.

Closing her eyes, Paige meditated on the short inspiration and whispered, "Thank you, Lord." Her lashes fluttered as a tear demanded out. She opened her eyes and released it. Taking a deep breath, she turned the page.

It's hard falling for someone, not knowing if he is the one. Seek God and give yourself space.

Remember, true love is caring about each other's souls.

Paige nodded and closed the book, opting not to write her thoughts in the space given for that. Before starting dinner, she texted her friend. Thanks. I needed this.

I know. That's what friends do—look out for each other. Love you, sister.

Lord, I only have one desire. Is Blake the one for me?

Master Sergeant Michaels glanced up when Blake marched into the U.S. Army recruiting office on a mission. "How was your training last weekend in St. Louis?" He offered Blake a seat in front of his desk.

Blake nodded. "That's why I'm back."

"I tried to talk you out of it," he said in a no-nonsense manner.

"I'm glad you didn't succeed. I'd like to request an interstate transfer from the Reserves to Missouri National Guard."

The recruiter's expression gave nothing away. A man wouldn't in his right mind uproot his life for a woman. Add God into the mix, and it seemed like Blake wasn't in his right mind. Paige seemed to have triggered something within him, desire for her and curiosity to understand God.

After shifting in his seat, Master Sergeant Michaels folded his hands and leaned across the desk. "Would you like to share your reasons for these unusual requests?"

Not wanting to hear more negative remarks, Blake gave him something logical. "The pay rate is better."

"That's your story, and you're sticking with it." He didn't wait for an answer. "I'll submit your request to Master Sergeant Lanier. You'll hear from him about his decision. In the interim, you are expected to honor your commitment to the reserves."

"Yes, sir." Blake said his goodbye. With nothing pressing, he cruised by familiar childhood hangouts, city landmarks, and popular eateries. He did the same ritual when his Ohio National Guard unit was deployed to Iraq. Years ago, he drove around conjuring up bittersweet memories. Back then, Blake didn't know if he would return home alive, maimed, suffering from post-traumatic stress disorder, or worse, with his remains in a flag-draped coffin. He gave a dry chuckle. He came back with some injuries, but he had survived.

I protected you! God corrected.

Blake didn't argue, but there were things God hadn't done that made his faith waver while in combat. The deaths of fellow soldiers was hard, but the passing of his grandmother was crushing.

When he was notified that his grandmother had suffered a stroke and it didn't look good, Blake had prayed that God would let her hold on until he got there. Blake's eyes watered, recalling how God had failed him. Granny Cross died while his plane was landing. Gritting his teeth, he pounded his fist on the steering wheel. Blake had been so close to seeing her alive one last time.

I died for her, so she could live again. I held your grandmother's hand when she took her last breath. I also was with you when your pilot became light-headed and I restored him to land the plane.

Blake swallowed, feeling as if God was giving him a spanking. After his grandmother's death, he had sugar coated his displeasure with God around family, but secretly, he was angry.

I knew and forgave you, God whispered.

How could God be merciful? Finding himself at Metroparks Lakefront, Blake parked and looked out into Lake Erie. For years, he thought he had suppressed his ill will against God. He would attend church if invited, but he had grown accustomed to building a fortress around his spirit that he wouldn't let the preachers penetrate. Paige had.

For the next couple of days, during his morning jogs, Blake kept questioning God. "What do you want from me, Lord?"

He heard nothing.

Then one night, after he had said his prayers and climbed into bed, he heard God's voice. *I need you in My army.*

Opening his eyes, Blake frowned. "What army?"

Read Ephesians six.

Scooting up in bed, he reached for his Bible. When he found the chapter, he began at verse one about children obeying their parents, then recalled Paige quoting bits and pieces from the same passage. Had he disrespected his father during their disagreement?

The tension between them was still tangible, but as his own man with his own mind, Blake refused to back down.

He loved his pops. Blake Sr. had always been his hero. It was time to make amends.

He was about to close his Bible, but he continued reading. Blake's heart pounded at verse eleven. *Put on the whole armor of God. That ye may be able to stand against the wiles of the devil.* Paige had mentioned armor.

Read, God prompted.

Blake finished the chapter. There wasn't enough arsenal in the world to win a war against an unseen enemy. He got it that he needed to suit up with truth, righteousness, the shield of faith, sword of the Spirit, the helmet of salvation... How was the gospel of peace a powerful weapon?

This is spiritual warfare, and I see the enemy Satan. He wants you, but I have prayed for you. Read Luke 22:31–32. Repent, Blake, and I will restore My relationship with you.

Blake did before closing his Bible and eyes to get some rest, but he tossed and turned all night. He welcomed the sunlight when it peeked through the blinds. As he pulled back the covers, Paige's ringtone made him smile.

"Are you up?" She sounded perky. "Sorry for dozing on you last night. Our team worked late to prepare interior samples for our client. I'm a little nervous. This client is challenging."

"Hey, God is with you"—and me too—"I'm sure you'll wow her with your expertise."

"Thank you for saying that." Her voice was shaky.

Blake wanted to say more to ease her anxiety, but she had to go. Plus, he had something that had to be taken care of immediately. After his morning regimen, he headed downstairs where his father was sitting in the kitchen sipping on coffee and staring out the patio doors. His mother had gone grocery shopping. "Hey, Pops."

His father nodded without looking Blake's way.

Taking a seat at the table, he cleared his throat. "Dad, I'm sorry about the other day. I shouldn't have used that tone. I respect you, I always have and always will."

The apology seemed to lift a heaviness off his father's face. "Does that mean you've reconsidered moving?"

"Nope." Shaking his head, Blake chose his words carefully. "I know my decision sounds crazy and not well thought out." He patted his chest. "It's the right choice for me. Paige is part of the reason, but not the total plan."

His father was quiet. "I see, but you can always come home."

Blake chuckled. "Dad, I'm thirty-four years old. I don't plan to come back home."

"I guess you're right." His father chuckled, then shrugged. Extending his hand, his dad shook on their reconciliation.

On Sunday, Blake attended Day of Pentecost Church again. He perked up when Pastor Kati Wyles referenced a battle from Second Kings 6:17. "God commands us to be strong in the power of His might. Israel thought they had nothing to fight with against the Syrian army." She paused and reread verse seventeen: *And the prophet Elisha prayed, and said, Lord, I pray thee, open his eyes, that he may see. And the Lord opened the eyes of the young man; and he saw: and, behold, the mountain was full of horses and chariots of fire round about Elisha...* Have you prayed today for the Lord to fight your battle?"

Blake didn't realize he had shaken his head.

Join my army today. I never lose a battle. My moves are strategic and everlasting, God whispered.

Too soon the pastor closed her Bible. "Your time is now. Repent by confessing your sins to God only. No one else needs to hear them. Make it personal, then come to the front where ministers will pray for you."

Blake didn't need more convincing. God had already invited him, so he was going to accept His complete plan of salvation. After the ministers prayed, Blake consented to the water baptism in Jesus' name.

Once he had changed out of his suit to a white T-shirt and pants, he stepped into the pool behind the pulpit. There was a man waiting in the water for the baptism. After following the minister's instruction to cross his hands over his chest, Blake closed his eyes.

"My dear brothers, upon the confession of your faith in the blessed Word of God, concerning His death, burial, and Grand Resurrection, I indeed baptize you in the mighty name of Jesus, for there is no other name under heaven whereby man must be saved according to Acts 4:12, for the remission of your sins and you shall receive the Holy Ghost. Amen."

Blake was submerged underneath. It felt as if he was drowning, dying in slow motion. Swimming was second nature to him, so why couldn't he save himself? Then in a flash, he re-emerged. Something was different as if he had been released from multiple strongholds. Involuntarily, Blake waved his hands in the air and shouted praises. A whirlwind of praises surrounded him, reminding Blake where he was.

Your crowd of witnesses. He heard God's voice seconds before he felt a spear of fire penetrate his soul. A heavenly language spilled from his mouth. God was speaking to him! His excitement could not be contained. Now, he understood Paige's allegiance to God. He couldn't wait to share this good news with her.

He worshiped God until practically all his strength was drained. Once he composed himself, the ministers led him back to the room where he dried off and changed into his clothes.

"Welcome home," Pastor Wyles greeted him in the hall. "You're a new creature. Keep eating God's Word, and you'll grow stronger every day."

"Thank you," he said in a hoarse voice.

"Our service is streamed over the internet, including on our Facebook page, so if you ever forget what God did for you today, watch it. You're dead to sin and are alive in Jesus. Of course, we don't show your face because of privacy concerns, but you can always tag yourself."

Blake didn't care who saw it. He'd experienced a spiritual high that he couldn't explain no matter how hard he tried. Before he could make it out of the parking lot, Blake worshiped the Lord in a dance without shame. Surprisingly, others joined in.

"Brother," one member said, patting his back, "praise God every chance you get."

"I will." Blake had to take several deep breaths to regulate his heart, then he thanked the man for the encouragement. Inside his car, he replayed what had happened. It was so unbelievable that he had to share the good news. Hopefully, Paige was either home from church or at her parents' house for dinner. He FaceTimed her.

"Hey." Her smiling face greeted him. "I was just thinking about you."

"Yeah?" Any other time he would have flirted or teased her. Not now. "Today," he began, choking, "God forgave me of my sins and filled me with the power of His Holy Ghost."

Paige screamed, "Hallelujah!"

"What happened?" Blake heard Paige's parents yell.

"Blake received the Holy Ghost!"

The power of God hit them too. He experienced a third round of worship with them. At thirty-four years old, Blake had experienced many things in life. This was all new to him.

"I wish I'd been there to witness it." Paige's yearning was evident as tears streamed down her cheeks and awe filled her voice.

"It's on Day of Pentecost Church's Facebook page."

"I'll call you back." She was gone before he could say goodbye.

Chapter 17

"You know this changes everything," Dominique said after they had watched the video. Once Paige left her parents, she made a visit to her friend's house unannounced. This news trumped protocol.

Thankfully, Dominique and Ashton were presentable to entertain guests.

"I know." Shaking her head, Paige whispered, "When I saw him rejoicing like that, my heart rejoiced."

"Girl," Dominique said, chuckling, "you're still rejoicing. You came into the house doing a happy dance. Ashton and I joined in."

Over the years, Paige had witnessed hundreds redeemed from their sins. With Blake, his salvation was so personal. She had kept him at two arm's length. She initially denied her attraction to him, but it thrived every moment they were in Charleston. Between God telling her to guard her heart, and Blake's masculine appeal, Paige knew better than to nurture what had started to bud in her heart so as not to fall into temptation. Dominique was right, Blake's conversion to a saint of God changed things. She reflected on her recent journal exercise, writing a Dear Future Husband love letter.

My Future Husband,

I've waited so long, hoping, praying, and crying that you were looking for me and that you would find me soon. God has kept me pure for you as the best gift I could offer you.

Please give me your best, especially your heart. I can't wait for us to hold hands, and for you to lead me, my godly husband, on our spiritual journey to heaven.

Sincerely,

Your wife in waiting

Her mind wandered as Dominique rambled on about double dating when Blake returned for reserves the following month.

Paige stood, coming out of her reverie. "I've got to go, sister, so I can call Blake back." She hugged both Dominique and Ashton goodbye and walked out to her car.

Once she was situated behind the wheel, Paige tapped his name on her phone. There were so many emotions swirling inside of her, she didn't know what to say first like *Am I the one for you?* Paige had to remind herself that Blake's salvation took priority. "How do you feel?"

"Honestly, like I'm ready to go to heaven."

A tear trickled down her cheek. That desire crossed many new converts' mind, to be as close to Jesus as possible. "I know. That's why maintaining God's holiness standards is our ticket out of this crazy world. I'm so happy for you." She sniffed. "You never talked about church, and I find out you've repented and were baptized in water and in the Spirit in the name of Jesus? I can't find the words right now. You never mentioned it."

He was quiet, and she didn't know what he was thinking or if he was going to answer. "I wasn't trying to impress you."

That stung. What woman didn't want a man to impress

her? She recovered from the hurt to appreciate the relationship he was developing with Christ. *I refuse to be wounded. Not today, Satan. This is a praise party, not a pity one.*

"Jesus had been dealing with me." He paused. "This was personal between me and the Lord."

His words were so tender that Paige knew God had drawn Blake with lovingkindness as He had said to his prophet in Jeremiah 31:3. "Amen," she whispered.

"Yes. Amen." The praise coming from his deep voice made her heart flutter. "Actually, I think your singles ministry clenched it for me. When I heard the sincerity in those brothers' answers, I wanted a walk with God like that, not only to impress you with a nurturing relationship but to have a confidence in God like never before."

She smiled. "We do have an awesome ministry at Salvation Temple. So I guess I'll see you the third weekend in October?"

"Sooner, if you want."

Paige's eyes brightened from her tears. "I don't want you to make a special trip—"

"What if I want to make it special?"

Closing her eyes, she allowed her heart to relish the moment. "Our annual hot air balloon race is held at the end of September."

"This weekend."

"Yes," she said. "You should see how beautiful—"

"I'll be there, and in time to attend the singles ministry," he added excitedly.

Her eyes teared. "I can't wait." Paige blew him a kiss.

He chuckled. "Caught it. Will you add a real hug to that when I see you?"

"You're pushing it," she teased, remembering the first

time Blake had asked for a hug. It was supposed to be goodbye, but it had been the beginning. They laughed together before ending the call.

The true test begins, God whispered, and her spirit plummeted. *You both have the power to resist the devil. Resist temptation.*

"Man, I still can't believe you're a viral sensation." Tucker couldn't stop laughing over the phone. "I thought I was watching some crazy man, but someone tagged you."

"Yes, it was me," Blake confirmed without shame. "That was my spirit pouring out God's praise. Jesus made a believer out of me. I heard this heavenly language spill from my mouth, twisting my tongue until it hurt afterward. It's real, man. I can testify that God is real."

"You didn't know that already?" Tucker grunted.

"I did, but," he paused, "God seemed so far removed from my everyday struggles that he became an afterthought to me."

"Did Paige brainwash you into this?"

"Watch it. She led me blindfolded to a place in God that I didn't believe existed."

His parents and sisters congratulated him on his conversion, but not without voicing some concerns. "You do realize we were already Christians," Monique said.

"How many Christians live it, sis?" He paused. "I carried the label like I picked a political affiliation, but my faith in God was weak. Blame it on the wars I fought." Blake patted his chest. "I'm ready to live it now."

"And moving to St. Louis is going to help you do that?"

Monique didn't back down while their mother remained silent.

Blake couldn't understand their pushback. Wanting a closer relationship with God was a positive change, yet they didn't see it like that. At one time, he didn't either. That was before he'd personally experienced God's power.

He hadn't heard back from the Missouri National Guard about his transfer request, but he doubted it would be a problem. Once it was official, he would tell Paige. In hindsight, Blake wished he hadn't given his family the heads-up of what he planned to do.

Blake continued steadfast with anything spiritual, especially reading his Bible. The best part now was he texted Paige scriptures.

One evening following dinner, he settled in front of his tablet to watch a movie on YouTube, but a Christian dating video on the sidebar caught his attention.

Until he moved to St. Louis, his relationship with Paige was limited to the phone. Seeing her, touching her, hugging, kissing… Blake rubbed his face. "God, help me." He read the part in the Bible where sexual immorality and fornication were sins against the body. His parents had drilled into him sex before marriage could result in a life-altering situation—a child.

For the most part, sex in Blake's past relationships was for mutual sexual gratification. He had fallen hard for one woman while serving in Iraq together. It wasn't long before Blake knew she wasn't the one for him to make a lifelong commitment.

Clicking on the video, Blake listened as a young minister discussed dating.

"Hey brothers, remember to keep Christ as the head in

your relationship. God first loved us, so set the example with your lady. Make sure you make her smile, not cry. She wants to feel important. Make sure she knows that every time you think about her, you're praying for her. Be patient, listen, send her a scripture or a short prayer throughout the day…" What captured Blake's attention was Minister Greg Haley, focused on the dos in a relationship, not the don'ts.

After watching a couple more of Minister Haley's videos, Blake subscribed to his channel. He forfeited the movie, opting to text Paige instead. Hey. Thinking about you. Working late?

Yes. The whole team is. Exhausted.

I'm praying for you. Call me when you get home, if not too tired.

I won't be.

Blake smiled. She was the only one who seemed to understand his spiritual rebirth.

He realized he had dozed off when her ringtone woke him.

"Hey. Sorry. Is it too late?"

He could hear the underlying tiredness in her voice. He longed to talk to her, but she needed her rest. She worked so hard on her projects, but she loved her job. "I wanted to make sure you got home safely. I don't like you working long hours and coming home late at night…I worry about you, so I pray."

"Prayer is all that matters. I'm looking forward to seeing the new you this weekend."

He chuckled. "And the new me can't wait to see you too. Good night."

Finally, it was Friday. Blake packed up his vehicle and headed for St. Louis. The thought of seeing Paige gave him an adrenaline rush as he drove on the interstate. Soon, the Gateway Arch, a recognizable St. Louis landmark served as a beacon to welcome him back.

This time, Blake booked a hotel near the airport, which wasn't far from Paige's church and her parents' house. Once he checked in, he texted Paige. Here in your Gateway City, or should I say the LOU. He had heard the term more than once when he was in St. Louis. It's after four. Should I hang here and meet you at church?

Finally! She texted back. Seems like forever since I saw you. Service is an hour earlier. We'll have prayer, then board the van for the Balloon Glow in Forest Park. I'm at Mom and Dad's. Come over.

Lord, I hope my salvation changed things with them and I'm not on the hot seat again.

With little traffic, Blake braced for impact twenty minutes later as he parked in front of Paige's parents' home. She was standing in the doorway like déjà vu. Her seductive eyes sparkled with happiness. Leaving her post, she met him halfway. "Blake," she whispered and fell into his arms, "I'm so happy for you."

"I'm happy for me too." He chuckled, squeezing her.

They stepped back and stared into each other's eyes, as if they both were contemplating their next move. "Come on, saint," she said with a ring to it.

To Blake's relief, Paige's family's reception this time was celebratory, as if he had returned from war.

"Welcome to the body of Christ," her father said with a wide grin, pumping his hand. The smile faded, and a frown appeared. "You're not off the hook with my daughter. I expect you to treat Paige as becoming of a godly man."

Blake nodded. Her father had no idea that Blake was

praying big time he didn't mess up this godly man thing, or he could lose everything—a real chance at winning Paige's heart, and weakening his newfound strong relationship with the Lord Jesus.

Chapter 18

Paige was about to explode with rejoicing over Blake's salvation. No wonder the Bible said in Luke 15:7 the angels rejoiced: *joy shall be in heaven over one sinner that repents, more than over ninety and nine just persons, which need no repentance.*

After enjoying her mother's beef brisket, mashed potatoes, and steamed vegetables, they talked about his spiritual re-birth, which her father called a Nicodemus experience. Finally, it was time for them to head to church.

"Why don't you ride for a change?" Blake jiggled his keys and opened the door for her.

She didn't argue as she slid into the passenger seat. His car smelled of his cologne and the new factory smell. Once he was behind the wheel, he faced her. "Do I have your permission to hold your hand?"

"Permission granted." It was the small things with this man that made her heart swell. His touch was strong but gentle.

Following her directions to the church, Blake turned to her. "There are a couple of things I didn't say to your family. I wanted to tell you first," he said, following her directions to the church.

She swallowed. *Uh-oh.* As she was about to withdraw her hand, he tightened his hold.

"I requested a transfer from the reserves to the Missouri National Guard. I received my letter this morning for a three-year commitment.

Paige blinked. "What are you saying?"

"I'm moving to St. Louis." He glanced at her while waiting at a light. "How do you feel about that?"

"I don't know," she said honestly. It was easy to resist temptation from her attraction when he was hundreds of miles away, but now?

"I was hoping you'd say that it's a good thing, and we can finish what we started in Charleston by dating—the Christian way." He grinned. "You already know I'm attracted to you, and it's been growing every time I hear your voice. Seeing you, I know my feelings will escalate." He paused and took a deep breath.

Tilting her head, she studied him. "What?"

"Knowing my limitations with you—sexually—is going to be a battle. I'm going to need your help."

His honesty scared her. She could only nod as she began to pray. *Lord, help us both.*

They were silent in their own thoughts until Blake said, "Can you help me house hunt?"

"Of course." She returned his smile. "Correct me if I'm wrong, but the National Guard isn't full-time, right?" Blake nodded, so Paige continued, "What are you going to do full-time?"

He chuckled and squeezed her hand. "One passion at a time. I have options. I can either use my G.I. Bill to return to school or find a civilian job, but it has to be one that will give me dual status, in case I'm activated."

"Which means?" She watched him, memorizing his expressions to recall when they spoke over the phone. Wait.

He was moving there, she reminded herself. They would get a chance to see each other more often. The excitement was settling in.

Blake rocked his head to the side, glancing at his rearview mirror. "Let's say I find a position as an accountant. If I'm called to active duty, my status will still be as an accountant, medic, technician, and stuff like that."

"I'm so excited you're here—will be here."

"Really?" He faced her and smiled. "I wasn't sure if you would consider that a good thing or not."

She was not about to tell him that his salvation had moved him up a notch with her. Yet, he had to learn how to walk godly, even if he wasn't the one her soul desired. Paige wouldn't be able to bear it if Blake wasn't the one for her. "St. Louis has some wonderful neighborhoods from the city to the county. Hazelwood, Bridgeton, Maryland Heights in Northwest County. U. City, Maplewood, and Richmond Heights are suburbs closer to the city. The choices are endless."

"Richmond Heights?" He smiled. "That will remind me of home. That's where I live now in the Cleveland area."

"Really?"

"Looks like we're starting to have more and more in common, my beautiful princess." He winked.

Once they arrived at church, Blake parked, and Paige waited for him to come around and open her door. Closing her eyes, she briefly breathed in the pampering. She wanted to continue to hold his hand, let him wrap his arm around her, and all those things couples in love did. *Whoa, you're going too fast*, Paige chimed herself. *Slow it down!*

So many times, she had walked into Salvation Temple for Friday night service, feeling like she had missed her turn at happiness. Tonight was different with Blake beside her. Minister Ray and the others who recognized Blake welcomed him back.

When Paige shared the good news about Blake receiving the water and fire baptism in Jesus' name, many of them rejoiced and danced without music. The uproar triggered the Holy Ghost inside of Blake. Paige began to worship, and praises ascended to the Lord.

Once the fifty-something members composed themselves, Minister Ray gave one last hand praise. "Whew, that is great news. I guess we've already prayed and praised God, so we can load up the vans. If you want to drive, stay close to the van. Brother and Sister Blake." He smiled, "Good ring to it. I'd encourage you to ride in the van or have another couple with you."

Minister Ray didn't have to say it, but Paige knew he was helping them to avoid temptation.

"I'll drive. I ride in enough group vans in the military," Blake explained.

Brother Meeks and Sister Cassie volunteered to ride with them. As expected, Art Hill in Forest Park was packed. They found available spots several blocks away.

"Wow. This is colorful." Blake reached for her hand and held on.

"Yes, and beautiful. The pilots fire up the balloons the night before the Great Forest Park Balloon Race. Against the night sky, the glow is spectacular.

"Tomorrow is just as exciting as the 'hound' balloons try to catch up with the Eveready 'hare' Bunny," Sister Cassie said.

"I like to come and watch the takeoff, but the real thing is, depending on where you are, you can see the balloons in the air for miles. We might be able to see them tomorrow while house hunting."

"Hopefully, something will be available for quick move-ins. I'm expected to report to duty in a couple of weeks."

The night's festivities and company created a perfect mood. She couldn't wait to tell Dominique and her cousins that Blake was moving to St. Louis.

The next morning, Paige waited until a decent hour—at least she hoped nine-thirty on a Saturday was enough time for married folks to wake up—before she called Dominique.

"Hold up," her friend said, sleep still in her voice. "This is happening way too fast for me. The Lord just filled him with the Holy Ghost and he's moving here?"

"Yep, and I'm taking him house hunting today." Paige giggled.

Dominique *umm-hmm*ed. "Ash and I don't have anything planned."

"I thought we were checking out the car sho—" her husband said in the background.

"Shhh, babe. I think we'll tag along. I don't want you two to get any ideas when you see the bedrooms."

"I think Blake and I can handle ourselves."

"Maybe so. God tells us to 'Be Ye Holy for I am Holy.'" She quoted First Peter 1:16. "Ashton and I are going to make sure of that. See you real soon. Bye."

Next, Paige called Claire, who screamed her excitement. "I'm surprised and not. I could tell he really liked you."

"How do you think Nyla is going to take it, considering things didn't work out with Blake's cousin?"

"That chick has moved on to a new love," Claire said. "I doubt she will care."

Minutes later, Paige called Nyla. "God saved Blake, and he's moving here."

At first, Nyla was quiet. "I hope it turns out better for you." It sounded like her cousin did care.

When Blake called, Paige was glad for the interruption. "I'll talk to you later." She clicked over. "Good morning, and praise the Lord!"

He chuckled, and his deep voice seemed to rumble. "Good morning to you, and yes, praise the Lord. What time do we begin our house-hunting excursion? I was hoping I could take you to breakfast."

She pouted. "Give me a rain check, but you'll get a chance to meet Dominique and her husband. They're going with us today. Be ready in an hour or so." She was about to end the call when Blake shared their morning scripture. *"Finally, brethren, whatsoever things are true, whatsoever things are honest, whatsoever things are just, whatsoever things are pure, whatsoever things are lovely, whatsoever things are of good report; if there be any virtue, and if there be any praise, think on these things.* Philippians 4:8. I thought of you."

"In what way?"

"I've been watching you, Paige, and listening to you from the very beginning. There was something about your confidence in Jesus that I want to practice. You're honest, possess a pure heart, and I believe I have found a virtuous woman."

"Wow." Paige teared. His words about her character were the best compliment she'd ever received from a man. "Thank you," she said softly. "See you soon." She praised God that Blake could see Jesus' light in her, then prayed, "Lord, even though my emotions are stirred, thank You for Your Word to keep me from falling."

And to present you faultless before the presence of My glory with exceeding joy. God whispered the remainder of His Word in Jude 1:24

It wasn't long before Dominique and Ashton arrived. After they exchanged hugs and kisses, Paige gushed. "I'm so excited for you to meet Blake."

"My wife says only the best for you, so I'm supposed to be hard on the brother." Ashton shook his head and squeezed Dominique. "Since he has the Holy Ghost, I'll step back and let the Lord lead him."

Dominique playfully elbowed him. "You're supposed to put the fear in him, so he'll know not mess over her…"

Paige waved her hand. "Trust me. Ben and Ray have that honor and have already laid down the rules." She reached for her jacket and purse, then scrutinized her appearance one more time before leaving.

Riding with the couple, Paige and Dominique chatted non-stop while Ashton drove, adding his two cents every now and then. Ashton was a great guy. When he and Dominique dated, he always included Paige on events, never making her feel like a third wheel.

Blake was outside sitting on a bench with his arms stretched across the back of it, and resting an ankle across his knee when they arrived at the Hilton. He stared into the sky as if he was tracking the planes coming in for a landing at the nearby Lambert Airport.

Ashton honked, and Paige waved until he recognized her. Standing, he began his trek toward the car.

Dominique said, "That hunk has got some serious swagger going on, and built…whew."

"Hey, aren't you married?" Paige teased.

"Yeah, am I not here?" Ashton asked.

Dominique leaned over and brushed a kiss on his lips. "I'll love you until my last breath, Mr. Taylor. My assessment is strictly looking out for my best friend with all that temptation."

"Good answer, wifey." Ashton stepped out of the car and shook Blake's hand. "What's up? Praise the Lord, brother."

Once Blake climbed in the backseat with Paige, her friend didn't wait for an introduction. "Hi. I'm Dominique. Paige's—"

"Best friend," Blake said. "I know."

"Man, they're something else," Ashton warned behind the wheel again and glanced in the rearview. "At least I won't be double-teamed now." He headed across town to the Richmond Heights area.

Blake took Paige's hand and seemed to study it before bringing it up to his lips. She wanted to faint from his gentleness. They held hands until they saw a house for sale on Wise Avenue. Ashton parked, and Blake helped her out of the car, then he stared into the sky at the balloons floating overhead.

"We thought about exchanging our vows in the air." Dominique sighed.

"That was all my wife's idea." Ashton shrugged. "I love her, so I was willing to go along for the ride." He snickered.

Dominique playfully bumped him. "The joke didn't work, dear. Anyhow, I changed my mind after a hot air balloon crashed a few years ago."

Minutes later, Paige and Blake walked the perimeter of the property while Dominique called the listing agent on the sign.

"This looks like a nice neighborhood. Would you live in

this community?" He asked Paige.

"I would." She twisted her lips. "It's a little pricey, but a great location to downtown, Clayton, and the city."

"Good to know." He squeezed her hand as Dominique and Ashton rejoined them.

"The agent said she usually doesn't show a house unless the buyer is pre-approved, but once I told her you are ex-army or marine—don't really know the difference—she changed her tune and said she would be here in less than half an hour," Dominique advised.

"Thanks." Blake nodded. "And for the record, the U.S. Army is twice the size of the marines." He smirked. "The Army's mission is to preserve the peace and security of the United States by defending it against any country's aggressive acts. The marines work with the navy."

"I stand corrected," Dominique paused and her expression changed.

What was her friend thinking? Paige wondered as Dominique squinted.

"Blake, I love Paige more than any of my sisters."

"You don't have any sisters," Paige reminded her.

"Exactly. Which is why she means everything to me. We've been together since we were teenagers. We've waited for the best gift God has for us. Ashton was my gift." She smiled at her husband. "Now, it's Paige's turn. She has been waiting a long time—impatiently—"

Paige scrunched up her nose. She was going to seriously hurt her friend. A car pulled up sooner than they expected. A woman stepped out, identifying herself as Tammy, the agent. She shook their hands and thanked Blake for his service.

As they followed Tammy inside, Blake whispered in her

ear, "I hear what your friend is saying, Paige, and you deserve the best—and I hope I'm perfect for you." He grinned. As soon as they entered the house, their heels echoed on the wood floor.

"Wow, this is magnificent." Paige was impressed.

"It's four bedrooms, updated kitchen, and baths." The woman paused. "When do you two need to move in?" She looked from Blake to Paige.

"Oh." Paige patted her chest and stepped back. "It's for him. He's relocating."

"Sorry," the agent said, clearly embarrassed from her assumption.

Blake pulled Paige to the side. "If you don't like it, I won't buy it."

Was she supposed to read between the lines that he was thinking permanency with her? Paige nodded and performed a more detailed tour, and praying with every step.

Chapter 19

That evening, Blake got a chance to know Paige's friends better as he accepted an invitation for a late fall barbecue at the Taylors' house. It was a casual atmosphere, and the meat was tender, falling off the bones. Paige and her friend seasoned the side dishes to perfection.

When Blake and Paige had a moment of privacy on the patio, he gathered Paige's hands in his. "I need you to know something." Blake stared into those bedroom eyes that still made him think about the bedroom, but as Paige's husband. "Okay, I'm just going to say this. I've been wounded in battle, and I've recovered… I'm invested in us. If I get wounded, I'm not sure if recovery is possible. My heart loves you, Paige Blake. It's not too soon to state the obvious, but I need a commitment from you to give us a try. You're one of the reasons I came for the drill. I had to see if there was a possible you and me." He paused. "Are you willing give you and me a try?"

He didn't mean to make her cry, but a tear fell. Her lips trembled as she tried to speak. Squeezing her hand, he wiped the tear with the other as he held his breath, waiting impatiently for her response. "It's okay. Talk to me, baby."

Paige exhaled. "No other man has ever said that to me before."

He lifted an eyebrow suspiciously. "As gorgeous as you are?"

She shook her head. "Not like you've said it, and I've felt it here." She patted her chest.

He gathered her into his arms and held her. *Lord, help me to love her as You want me to,* he prayed.

Minutes after his declaration, she had whispered, "And it's not too soon for me to know how you feel. I love you, too, and I thought I might not ever get a chance to say that."

He couldn't resist his tease. "I knew you did."

She playfully shoved him away. "And how did you know it?"

"Let me just say, my heart knew it."

"Ashton and I both knew too," Dominique said as they rejoined them on the patio. Evidently, Paige's friend had perfect hearing. With Paige cuddled under his arm on one short sofa and the newlyweds on another, they discussed Bible passages, Cleveland, what St. Louis had to offer, and the military.

Blake took those memories back to Cleveland with him, and now, he couldn't wait to make St. Louis home, especially after he heard Sunday's message at Paige's church.

"We don't always see our enemies. They don't always carry physical weapons." The pastor paused and tapped a finger on his chin. "Ever heard the saying, 'Sometimes we are our worse enemy?' I would say Biblically, it's true if—and that is a big if—we aren't led by the Spirit of Christ. Galatians 5:16 says, Walk in the Spirit, and ye shall not fulfill the lust of the flesh. For the flesh lusts against the Spirit, and the Spirit against the flesh: and these are contrary the one to the other: so that ye cannot do the things that ye would.' This is a war we can't win without Jesus. The flesh will get you in trouble, killed, and even deposited in hell. Look at what the flesh can do in verse nineteen through twenty-one…"

After service, Blake took Paige to a late brunch. They

discussed the three houses they were able to view the day before, the sermon and scriptures. "I'm not taking you, our relationship, or my salvation lightly." He was flustered. "But this is new to me. Pray for me and us."

"I will." She had reached across the table, covered his hands with hers, and did just that.

That prayer—her prayer—had staying power during his drive back to Cleveland until he parked at his parents' house. Collapsing on his bed, he was too tired to get up and shower, but that didn't stop him from sliding to his knees to petition God himself. Before drifting off to sleep, he summoned his lady's flawless face and smiled. "Every man needs to have a praying woman."

The next day while working with a loan officer for a loan preapproval, Blake received his orders to report for duty at Fort Leonard Wood, Missouri, a which was a couple of hours from St. Louis, in twelve days. He had hoped to be assigned to the location at the St. Louis airport, but either way, he would be closer to Paige.

When Blake had separated from the army, he was unsure of his next move in life until a chance meeting with an incredible woman started him on a mission to commit his life to Christ. He thought he was pursuing Paige, but she had been a light to point him to The Light.

A week later, on the day of Blake's move, his sisters took off work to give him tearful goodbyes.

Blake groaned as he towered over Monique and Sanette in a group hug similar to the one twelve years ago when his unit was activated. "You two are acting like I'm getting deployed sixty-two hundred miles to Iraq. St. Louis is less than six hundred miles away."

"Perfect, which is why we're planning a road trip next

weekend." Monique curled her lips upward and folded her arms. "Do you think we're going to let any chick steal our baby brother from us?"

Blake groaned and shook his head. He wasn't about to tell them Paige had stolen his heart with one look. If anything, he needed to keep the Blakes and Crosses separate over their baby girl and baby boy issues.

"We'll make our own assessment," Sanette chimed in with a game face.

Blake looked to his dad for rescue.

"You're on your own." His father walked into the kitchen. Blake heard his snicker.

Great. Blake anchored his hands on his waist. "I'm no longer a baby. I haven't been since I was potty trained."

"Are you going to live with Paige?" Sanette asked.

"Not without rings on our fingers. Otherwise, we both run the risk of living forever in hell. I'm going to be in an extended stay hotel until I put a contract on a house in Richmond Heights, Missouri." They peppered him with questions until he recognized their stall tactics, and he announced it was time to go. Blake shook hands with his father and hugged his teary-eyed mother and got on the road. He didn't exhale until he was behind the wheel and exited onto I-71 South.

The following week, true to his sisters' threats, his family arrived in St. Louis, under the guise of making sure he was safe. It was comical.

"I'm not just talking about the neighborhood." Sanette lowered her voice, "I want to make sure your heart is safe. How soon can we meet Paige?"

"It's already been arranged."

"Really? When?" Monique demanded.

"The Blakes have invited us to dinner tomorrow." Blake folded his arms. Checkmate.

The next day, Paige was nervous as she raided her closet for the perfect outfit to meet Blake's family. Dominique was on the speakerphone, guiding her.

"Wear that green and blue sweater dress. It will accent your eyes."

"Okay." Paige couldn't keep her heart from pounding. It was a good thing she was able to get a hair appointment on Friday after work. She was there for four hours, but the manicure, facial, and hair treatment were worth it. "His parents seemed nice, but then again, I wasn't in a good frame of mind." She didn't tell Dominique that it was the night she had a meltdown after witnessing a wedding at the hotel. Paige didn't want her friend to know how devastated she had felt. "I saw one of his sisters from afar. She didn't look mean." She gnawed on her lips.

"Do Ashton and I need to invite ourselves over to your folks' house? Say the word, and I'm on it."

Paige chuckled. Her friend was a mama bear before becoming a mother. "No. I'm sure I'm overreacting. Let me finish getting dressed."

"Okay, sister. I'll pray everything will work out. Their barks are probably bigger than their bites. Love you. Bye."

An hour later, she arrived at her parents' house where her brothers, their wives, and her nephew were in a jovial mood. After hellos and hugs, she received a text from Blake.

ETA. 5 minutes. Love you.

Yeah, she loved him too. Was it enough? Paige hoped so as she peeked out the window until Blake parked his SUV in front of the house. Two other cars trailed him. She swallowed, smoothed down her dress, and opened the door like she normally did when waiting on Blake.

Bright smiles from Blake and his parents relaxed her. His sisters' unreadable expressions concerned her. While Blake made the introductions, Paige extended her hand. His mother immediately wrapped her in a hug.

"Hello, dear. It's good to see you again." Mrs. Cross' eyes twinkled.

After his father, next came his sisters. "Paige, these are my sisters, Monique and Sanette, and their husbands."

"Hello." Paige nodded as Blake stayed near her side.

Blake's oldest sister leaned closer. "One question, maybe two, depending on answer number one."

"Monique," Blake raised his voice. She ignored her brother and lifted an eyebrow. "Did you encourage my brother to move here?"

Paige frowned. "No." She shook her head as Blake reached for her hand and squeezed it. "I believe everyone else knew before me."

"Hmm-mm. Do you love him—I mean really love him?" She squinted. "Because I hope that's the only way he'll stay."

"That's easy." Paige grinned and gazed into Blake's eyes. She saw pure love in them. "Yes."

"I had to double-check." Monique walked ahead and met the rest of the Blake family.

Paige exhaled and collapsed in the hug Blake had waiting for her. "Whew." She and Blake braced for hostile fire that never came, to her relief.

"Love conquers all, babe. It conquers everything," he cooed against her ear.

Chapter 20

"This is not how I envisioned Blake and me spending time together," Paige complained to her cousin Claire who called her every week for updates and was disappointed that Paige wasn't wearing a ring and shopping for a wedding dress. "It seems like he's been gone longer than three weeks for training." Despite the separation, their relationship budded.

Claire laughed. "I see God working this out for your good."

"In what way?" Paige asked as she stretched out on her sofa to watch a sitcom.

"This separation is possibly God's way to keep you two holy. Blake knows you're there for him, and you know he's there for you. I hope one day I can say that."

Her cousin's sadness was so familiar. "Like we've told each other over the years, your day is coming," Paige said, trying to encourage her.

"Yeah. So how many more weeks before Mr. Blake is set free?"

"In seven weeks. Ten days before Christmas. His APFT training—I'm learning all these military terms…" She smiled. "The Army Physical Fitness Test has been rough on him. He said the couple of months out of active duty set him back."

A week later on Veteran's Day, Paige wanted to do more than enjoying the day off work by cleaning the house or taking advantage of the holiday bargains. It had a greater meaning since she was now in love with a veteran.

With Ashton and Dominique enjoying the holiday together, Paige decided to drive to Jefferson Barracks National Cemetery, about thirty miles away. Although she hadn't attended many gravesite services, her parents didn't skip them. They said it was important to go "the last mile of the way," with family and friends from the funeral and to the burial.

Paige didn't expect to see several funeral processions on a holiday, especially on the day to honor veterans. Parking her car to the side, she got out and noted the endless bleach white tombstones aligned in precision rows. The history of the cemetery was posted nearby. She blinked at the number of remains gathered there—almost two hundred thousand.

What better way to honor Veterans Day than to remember those who died, she thought as she took off across the road and strolled aimlessly through neat aisles.

She glanced at one headstone: Mark Winn, Sergeant, U. S. Army, WWII and June 7, 1926–June 7, 2006. "He died on his birthday?" That made his death even sadder to her.

She kept walking until something drew her to an older part of the cemetery where the tombstones were worn. There were hundreds of remains of soldiers from the U.S. Colored Infantry who fought in the Civil War. She thought about her conversation with Blake about ultimate sacrifices.

Their remains were a testament to their willingness to die for a cause. As a result of their sacrifice, Paige had the freedom for the most part, to attend any college, earn a nice salary, and live where she could afford in spite of her skin color. She still maintained the best and true ultimate sacrifice was Jesus dying on a tree to take her to a place where there wouldn't be any wars ever, ever again.

Paige shivered standing in the valley of death. Maybe this field trip wasn't a good idea. As she thought about returning to her car, it seemed as if tombstones were begging her to acknowledge them. There were so many wars. She stopped at the gravesite of Heary Joe Eastern Jr., Private, U. S. Army, September 3, 1981–April 30, 2000. Her heart sunk. He was just a baby.

My will is perfect, God whispered. *If in this life only you have hope, you are among the most miserable. This man's hope was in Me.*

She blinked, accepting God's perfect will. Glancing in another direction, the tombstone of Sarah H. Ransom caught her eye.

Her hope was in Me.

Moving from grave to grave, Paige listened for God's voice. Sometimes He spoke. Other times, He remained silent. Back at her car, Paige saluted the fallen soldiers.

A loud boom above caused her to look up. She expected to see a fighter jet in the sky. There wasn't any sign of one coming or going.

I suffered a brutal death, but I rose triumphant. One day, I will descend from heaven with a shout, with the voice of the archangel, and the dead who are buried in My name shall rise first. Then those who are alive shall be caught up with them in the clouds, to meet Me. God whispered the words of First Thessalonians 4:16–17.

Paige returned to her car, reciting verse eighteen: *Comfort one another with these Words.*

She smiled as she drove away. "Yes, Lord. I'm waiting for Your return. Can I get married and have children first?"

She didn't expect God to answer, and He didn't.

Later that evening, Blake called her. She answered with, "Hey, I miss you."

"I miss you more," Blake said. "Although boot camp is intense, I'm weak from missing you. I love you so much, Paige. Don't doubt it."

"I don't. I visited Jefferson Barracks National Cemetery earlier as a way to honor veterans, and to think about your sacrifice."

"Thank you," he said softly, then became quiet. "I wonder if I'd have re-enlisted three times if we had met sooner."

"God's timing is perfect. I'm glad we met when we did," she told him.

"Me too." He threw her a kiss over the phone. "Okay, you've been my five minutes of distraction, so I could concentrate on completing the rest of my training. Love you."

"I love you," she whispered. Before ending the call, they shared a scripture, prayer, and smacked a loud kiss on the phone.

Blake's graduation was better than any company Christmas party Paige had ever attended. It was a family celebration with the Cross and Blake families. Once the troops were dismissed, Paige made a beeline for him. How did wives and girlfriends bear months and years of separation after they had found the other half of their heart? When he saw her, his eyes lit up. She ran toward him. He met her halfway and wrapped his arms around her.

She saluted him with her hand when she wanted to share their first kiss with a passion that had been bottled up for the right moment. Unfortunately, it still wasn't the right moment with so many spectators around, but if they had some privacy that might not be good either.

His eyes burned with fire. "You know I want to kiss you."

"And I want to kiss you back." Paige's eyes misted.

"We're going to make that happen." Blake winked at the same time he was swarmed with congratulations.

Blake didn't break eye contact with Paige as he mouthed, *One day.*

Chapter 21

Paige's father greeted Blake at the door. "Good evening, sir." Blake removed his cap and accepted a handshake before he was invited inside. "Thank you for seeing me."

Her father nodded as his wife appeared. "I hope you're hungry. I have a pot roast ready." She smiled, and Blake saw a glimpse of Paige.

"I guess I'd better make this quick because I know you won't feed me until after the interrogation."

Mrs. Blake laughed; her husband didn't. "You're catching on." Mr. Blake folded his arms and leaned forward. His body language said, "Bring it."

So Blake did. "I love Paige with everything Christ has instilled within me. She's good for me, and I want to be good to and for her. I'm asking for your blessings to trust me with your baby girl…" Blake saw her as a beautiful woman, but he had to speak the family's jargon so they would know he understood how much Paige meant to them. He didn't exhale until he finished pouring out his soul.

Of all people, especially Paige's father, Blake didn't think he'd hear a grown, fearless man break down. The moment had caused moisture to gather in his eyes too. Mrs. Blake was the only somber one trying to comfort them both.

"Paige means the world to me—us. No man has ever been good enough for my daughter—ever. When I saw you talking with my daughter in the hotel lobby, my wife stopped me from breaking it up. I sent my son to do the dirty work." That earned him a punch in his arm from his wife.

Blake reined in his amusement.

"But God has reshaped your life. I see you are in the Lord's army now, and I believe you'll protect my daughter and be a good husband, so yes, I would be honored to have you as my son-in-law."

When Blake heard the word *honored,* he lost it. He leaped to his feet and praise spilled from his mouth. He didn't count how many hallelujahs he shouted, but his voice was hoarse afterward.

That evening, back in his newly purchased home, which had nothing more than a bedroom set, Blake's heart pounded with excitement as he phoned his parents.

"I'm going to propose. I have Paige's father's blessings." While his father gave him hearty congratulations and words on how to be a good husband, Blake had to remove the phone from his ear when his mother screamed for joy. Once she gained composure, Blake said, "I was hoping you would come in town and help me."

To say Lily Cross was happy to get a daughter-in-law was an understatement. She had jumped at the chance to have a hand in helping to create a perfect setting for his proposal. "This is the best Christmas present you could give me— well, next to a new grandbaby," she had told him over the phone.

"Let me get my wife first."

His heart swelled with happiness after talking to his parents. He praised the Lord for putting Paige in that elevator at that day and time. Their steps had been truly orchestrated by God.

I established your steps, and I will hold on, so you will not fall, God whispered.

He wondered if that was a passage in his Bible. Usually, God directed him. He located Psalm 37:23–25. The words had been so powerful that he called and shared them with Paige. She had no idea why and who had prompted him to read them.

Fast-forward to tonight, and Blake double-checked his appearance. Everything was in place for him to propose.

He called his parents who were staying at the Holiday Inn nearby. "Mom, I'm leaving now. You have one hour to pull this together. You have my spare house key, right?"

"Son, we've got this—Paige's mom, her sisters-in-law, your sisters, and me. You just go and get you a fiancée."

"Will do." He took a deep breath, grabbed his coat and keys, and began the journey that would change his life before the night was over. Paige was at her parents' house waiting for him to take her to dinner. Although they had been dating for months and Blake had Paige's address, they thought it best for him not to visit her alone. Their passion, hormones, and love was too powerful for them to succumb to sin.

As he parked at the curb a half hour later, his heart pounded. Blake was fearless in serving his country, yet he was scared of his little woman. He patted his pocket, double-checking the ring box was still there.

Blake wasn't disappointed as Paige opened the door, waiting for his arrival. As he walked closer, her hazel eyes glistened under the porch light and seemed more seductive. He exhaled and dismissed the worldly thoughts. This night was about honoring her and God.

"Hey." She reached out and hugged him.

Lifting her off her feet, he hugged her back while stepping into the house. Releasing her, he spoke to William and Miranda Blake. Their faces gave nothing away of what was about to come, even though they had their coats on. Their excuse was riding around to enjoy the Christmas lights, then having dinner.

"Enjoy your dinner," her father said as Blake helped Paige with her coat.

Once they were in the car, Blake didn't start the engine. Instead of driving off, he took in her beauty. They were seldom alone. His senses were on high alert from her hazel eyes, perfume, and hair, which was crowned with a hat to keep her warm from the Arctic blast in St. Louis.

"What?"

"Can't I take a few minutes and admire my beautiful lady?" He was also giving her family a head start to their destination as they walked out the house and waved at them.

"Yes." Paige lost the battle at blushing. "So where are you taking me for dinner?'

"It's a surprise." He grabbed her hand, squeezed it, then started his engine once he saw the taillights of her parents' car.

Smiling, he drove off slowly. *Jesus, I love her. I really love her. Help me never to disappoint You or her,* he prayed silently.

He tapped his radio, and jazz music serenaded them until they were within miles of their destination.

She chuckled. "We're in Clayton. You know you could have taken the highway."

"Yeah, but I like the scenic route this time of year," he said as he parked in front of The Crossings Restaurant minutes later.

Paige perked up and glanced around. "Oh, I've never eaten here."

"Me either." The restaurant was only a cover to throw her off. He paused and reached in the backseat. "Do you trust me?" He dangled a white handkerchief in front of her, and the fear that covered her face made him rethink his stunt.

"I…ah." She frowned. "It all depends."

"Sweetheart, I need you to trust me a little." He used his thumb and finger to demonstrate.

"O-okay," she said in a shaky voice.

He could kick himself for causing her to fear him. This was what she desired, a godly man who she could trust to blindfold her. Slowly, she consented.

Lovingly, Blake tied the blindfold around her eyes. "You okay? Is this too tight?"

"No," she whispered.

He brushed a soft kiss against her cheek, then reached in the backseat and handed her his first engagement gift. He rested the book in her lap. She fingered it. "A Bible?"

"Yes. Before we eat, I need to show you something."

"You have me blindfolded, so how can I see anything?"

"You've got me." Blake pulled off and headed toward his house on Wise Avenue in Richmond Heights. When they arrived, Blake looked down the street. Headlights flashed, signaling everything was ready. Going around the car, he guided Paige out and steadied her on the sidewalk. After positioning Paige to face the house, he took a deep breath. "Ready?"

"Yes." She shivered, and he removed the handkerchief.

She gasped. "The house!" She looked at him. "When did you…"

"I closed on it a week ago." He grinned. She thought he had put house buying on hold until he finished boot camp. During one of their short phone calls, she told him the for-sale sign was gone, and someone had bought it.

"How? You've been on active duty."

"I had my paperwork notarized online and had the closing costs transferred from my bank." Blake took Paige's arm to lead her up the stairs, but she hesitated.

"Ah, Blake." She faced him. "You asked if I trusted you," Paige nodded. "I do, but I don't trust our attraction. There's too much temptation behind those closed doors."

Blake squeezed her hand. "There could be blessings on the other side. I will always protect your heart and soul." He thought about the questions and answers from the singles ministry's Dating Game.

After taking a deep breath, she consented and they proceeded up the stairs. Blake's heart pounded as he opened the door. "Wow," escaped their lips at the same time. In his opinion, the ladies in their families had created a cozy atmosphere to rival any five-star establishment.

Blake helped Paige slip off her coat, then he removed his and tossed it over a railing. He escorted her to the chair that was elegantly decorated with an overkill of fancy ruffles on the skirt. "Open your Bible."

Paige did and whimpered as she fingered the engraved message. "To Paige Blake from Blake Cross. Thank you for showing me the love of Christ." She looked at him with teary eyes. "Thank you for loving me," she whispered.

"One thing you said never escaped me. You wanted trust

from your man—godly man—and I've prayed hard to honor you and earn your trust. I felt so bad when I saw the fear on your face when I produced the handkerchief, and that hurt me, but you said, quote 'I want to close my eyes, be blindfolded and take my husband's hand, because I trust him to lead as Christ gives him directions.'"

A tear trickled down her cheek, and he caught it. "I listened. Babe, I have a heart that can be broken, too, and I trust you. I don't believe you will let me get hit by a car, fall, or whatever. So I ask you, do you trust me?"

"Yes. No doubts." She beamed.

"Good answer," he said as he got down on one knee. "I need another answer." He dug into his pocket and pulled out the box. "Paige Blake, you're a part of my heart." He patted his chest. "You've been carrying my name since the day you were born, so I'm here asking you to be my wife and carry my name until our last breaths."

"Yes, yes." Standing, she wrapped her arms around his neck and they shared their first kiss as an engaged couple.

Paige was in a daze. The tears didn't help. Her lips protested when Blake broke away.

"One more thing," Blake whispered, twirling her around until he guided her to sit again, pulled out a box from his other pocket, and handed it to her. He seemed to be amused by her bewilderment.

"From reading my Bible, I understand the importance of an engagement. In Mary and Joseph's case, and the passage about the ten virgins, the engagement is as sacred as the marriage, so until we're married—sooner I hope rather than later—I want to wear this ring as my commitment to you and to let others know that I belong to you."

In awe that Blake had the desire to seek a deeper understanding of commitment from a Biblical standpoint, she complied with slipping the ring on his finger. Her heart fluttered as she placed her hands on both sides of his face and stared into his eyes. As he inched closer, she met him to indulge in their second sweet kiss of commitment. Would she always count their kisses?

Standing, he pulled Paige to her feet and twirled her around, quoting a scripture. *"Men ought to love their wives as their own bodies. He that loves his wife loves himself. For no man ever yet hated his own flesh; but nourishes and cherishes it, even as the Lord does the church."*

"Wait until I tell Dominique."

"You don't have to." He walked to the window and opened the blinds. Within minutes, the door burst open, and her family and friends poured into the house: Dominique and Ashton, her family, and Claire had flown into town, along with Nyla. They hugged and congratulated her first, then she and Blake switched sides, and his family welcomed her. She was surprised that Tucker had come too, and he and Nyla weren't at each other's throat.

"You sure took a long time to propose, son," his mother scolded. "We almost froze out there waiting for the signal."

"Let's eat," her brother Benjamin said. "All this waiting has made me hungry."

As if on cue, their catered food arrived, along with small tables and chairs.

Dominique pulled her aside. "You know how Ashton proposed, so I want to hear all the details."

"And you will, but first, I have to grab my fiancé." Paige closed her eyes and screamed, silencing the room. "I'm engaged!"

Epilogue

aige and Blake had decided on a Valentine's Day wedding, but when his unit was activated to assist the guardsmen in California for a natural disaster, they moved it to an April spring wedding, then his tour was extended another forty-five days. So now, the third time was a charm, and they made plans for a summer wedding, even if they had to have Skype nuptials.

Mark 10:8 took on a new meaning for Paige and Blake. "The two shall be one flesh: so then they are no more two." It took finagling and prayer, but the Blakes and Crosses and Crofts and Bells agreed to return to The DoubleTree Hotel in Charleston on the same weekend for joint family reunions and their wedding.

God seemed to hold back any calamities that would take Blake away, so now their families filled the courtyard with standing room only. The interior designer in Paige hoped safety precautions were in place for easy exits. Today, she would turn her mind off and only think about becoming Blake's wife.

Dominique was her matron of honor, Blake's sisters were bridesmaids, as well as Paige's cousins Claire and Nyla. Mr. Cross was Blake's best man. Blake had said he wouldn't have anyone else but his father, and Paige agreed. Their fathers had been towers of strength in their lives, so it only made sense for her father to give her away and Blake's father to be on the other side when she took her vows.

When Paige insisted Blake have some single groomsmen, he complied with Tucker, another cousin, then his brothers-in-law.

Even Minister Ray and his wife flew into Charleston for the occasion and to officiate the ceremony.

As Paige glided closer to the front on her father's arm, her eyes locked with Blake who was handsome in his formal military uniform. The faint smile hinted that he was pleased with what he saw. Her eyes misted. God had not forsaken her.

My timing is perfect, the Lord whispered.

"Thank You, Jesus," she whispered back.

As her father handed her off to Blake, his voice cracked. "Take care of her."

"God is my witness, I will."

Standing in front, staring into Blake's eyes seemed surreal. Although she couldn't wait to take his name, Paige was nervous and couldn't stop shaking. She was taking deep breaths to calm her anxiety as she recited her vows in between Blake mouthing, "Trust me."

"You may now salute your bride," Minister Ray announced.

Paige waited for their lips to touch and seal their commitment. Her vision blurred as she closed her eyes to experience their kiss. It was as explosive as the thunderous applause.

"Never forget I love you," he whispered against her lips.

"Never."

No doubt the kiss was memorable. Now, she couldn't

wait for the first dance with her new husband. As the quartet began to play the music, Blake stood and reached for her hand. Once they were in the center, he winked and twirled her around under his arm. Closing her eyes, Paige enjoyed the moment. When he guided her to his chest, his nostrils flared as he stared deeply into her eyes. He kissed her again, and they danced even after the music finished, then he dipped her. When she straightened up, he ended it with another kiss to the applause of the guests.

On their way back to the table, Blake's aunt Myrtle intercepted their path with her cane.

"Welcome to the family, sugar. You keep him in line. You have to train these knuckleheaded Cross men… now I expect to see a little Cross at the next reunion. I added a spot for him, her, or both on the family tree."

Blake winked. "We'll see what we can do." He faced Paige and tickled her ear with his breath.

Who knows, Paige thought, next year the Blakes might have a late summer baby to play with the one Dominique would deliver in early spring.

Thank you so much for reading. I hope you've enjoyed *Late Summer Love,* book two of the Perfect Chance at Love series. Will you take a few minutes to post a review and tell a friend? Who's next to have a perfect chance at love? Find out by signing up for my monthly newsletter at patsimmons.net.

Until next time, be blessed!

Pat

Book Club Discussions

1. Talk about places you least expect to find a love connection.
2. Discuss the sacrifices mentioned in the story.
3. How do you honor Jesus' sacrifice compared to veterans?
4. What was your favorite scripture in *Late Summer Love*?
5. How do you spend your Veterans Day?
6. Talk about Dominique and Paige's friendship.
7. Share some fun things about your family reunion.

About the author...

Pat Simmons has celebrated ten years as a published author with more than thirty titles. She is a self-proclaimed genealogy sleuth who is passionate about researching her ancestors and then casting them in starring roles in her novels.

She is a three-time recipient of the Romance Slam Jam Emma Rodgers Award for Best Inspirational Romance. Pat describes the evidence of the gift of the Holy Ghost as an amazing, unforgettable, life-altering experience.

Pat holds a B.S. in mass communications from Emerson College in Boston, Massachusetts. She has worked in various media positions for more than twenty years. Currently, she oversees the media publicity for the annual RT Booklovers Conventions.

She has been a featured speaker and workshop presenter at various venues across the country and converted her sofa-strapped sports fanatic husband into an amateur travel agent, untrained bodyguard, GPS-guided chauffeur.

Readers may learn more about Pat and her books by connecting with her on social media, www.patsimmons.net, or by contacting her at authorpatsimmons@gmail.

Other Christian titles include:

The Guilty Jamieson Legacy series
Book I: *Guilty of Love*
Book II: *Not Guilty of Love*
Book III: *Still Guilty*
Book IV: *The Acquittal*
Book V: *Guilty by Association*
Book VI: *The Guilt Trip*
Book VII: *Free from Guilt*
Book VIII: *The Confession*

The Carmen Sisters
Book I: *No Easy Catch*
Book II: *In Defense of Love*
Book III: *Driven to Be Loved*
Book IV: *Redeeming Heart*

Love at the Crossroads
Book I: *Stopping Traffic*
Book II: *A Baby for Christmas*
Book III: *The Keepsake*
Book IV: *What God Has for Me*
Book V: *Every Woman Needs a Praying Man*

Making Love Work Anthology
Book I: *Love at Work*
Book II: *Words of Love*
Book III: *A Mother's Love*

Restore My Soul series
Crowning Glory

Jet: The Back Story
Love Led by the Spirit

Perfect Chance at Love series:
Love by Delivery
Late Summer Love

Single titles
Talk to Me
Her Dress (novella)
Christmas Greetings
Couple by Christmas
Prayers Answered by Christmas
Anderson Brothers
Book I: Love for the Holidays (Three novellas): *A Christian Christmas, A Christian Easter, and*
A Christian Father's Day
Book II: *A Woman After David's Heart (Valentine's Day)*
Book III: *A Noelle for Nathan* (Book 3 of the Andersen Brothers)

PERFECT CHANCE AT *Love* SERIES

Love by Delivery
PAT SIMMONS

In *Love by Delivery*, Senior Accounts Manager Dominique Hayes has it all money, a car and a condo. Well, almost. She's starting to believe love has passed her by. One thing for sure, she can't hurry God, so she continues to wait while losing hope that a special Godly man will ever make his appearance. Package Courier Ashton Taylor knows a man who finds a wife finds a good thing. The only thing standing in his way of finding the right woman is his long work hours. Or maybe not. A chance meeting changes everything. When love finally comes knocking, will Dominique open the door and accept Ashton's special delivery?

In *Late Summer Love*, it takes strategies to win a war, but prayer and spiritual intervention are needed to win a godly woman's heart. God has been calling out to Blake Cross ever since Blake was deployed in Iraq and he took his safety for granted. Now, back on American soil, Blake still won't surrender his soul--until he meets Paige Blake during a family reunion. When the Lord gives Blake an ultimatum, is Blake listening, and is he finally ready to learn what it takes to be a godly man fit for a godly woman?

In *Crowning Glory,* **Book 1**, Cinderella had a prince; Karyn Wallace has a King. While Karyn served four years in prison for an unthinkable crime, she embraced salvation through Crowns for Christ outreach ministry. After her release, Karyn stays strong and confident, despite the stigma society places on ex-offenders. Since Christ strengthens the underdog, Karyn refuses to sway away from the scripture, "He who the Son has set free is free indeed." Levi Tolliver, for the most part, is a practicing Christian. One contradiction is he doesn't believe in turning the other cheek. He's steadfast there is a price to pay for every sin committed, especially after the untimely death of his wife during a robbery. Then Karyn enters Levi's life. He is enthralled not only with her beauty, but her sweet spirit until he learns about her incarceration. If Levi can accept that Christ paid Karyn's debt in full, then a treasure awaits him. This is a powerful tale and reminds readers of the permanency of redemption.

Jet: The Back Story to Love Led By the Spirit, Book 2, to say Jesetta "Jet" Hutchens has issues is an understatement. In *Crowning Glory,* Book 1 of the Restoring My Soul series, she releases a firestorm of anger with an unforgiving heart. But every hurting soul has a history. In *Jet: The Back Story to Love*

Led by the Spirit, Jet doesn't know how to cope with the loss of her younger sister, Diane.

But God sets her on the road to a spiritual recovery. To make sure she doesn't get lost, Jesus sends the handsome and single Minister Rossi Tolliver to be her guide.

Psalm 147:3 says Jesus can heal the brokenhearted and bind up their wounds. That sets the stage for *Love Led by the Spirit.*

In *Love Led by the Spirit,* Book 3, Minister Rossi Tolliver is ready to settle down. Besides the outwardly attraction, he desires a woman who is sweet, humble, and loves church folks. Sounds simple enough on paper, but when he gets off his knees, praying for that special someone to come into his life, God opens his eyes to the woman who has been there all along. There is only a slight problem. Love is the farthest thing from Jesetta "Jet" Hutchens' mind. But Rossi, the man and the minister, is hard to resist. Is Jet ready to allow the Holy Spirit to lead her to love?

LOVE AT THE CROSSROADS SERIES

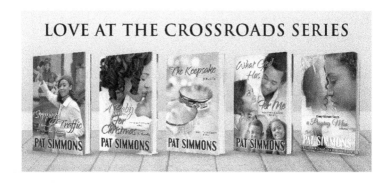

In *Stopping Traffic*, Book 1, Candace Clark has a phobia about crossing the street, and for good reason. As fate would have it, her daughter's principal assigns her to crossing guard duties as part of the school's Parent Participation program. With no choice in the matter, Candace begrudgingly accepts her stop sign and safety vest, then reports to her designated crosswalk. Once Candace is determined to overcome her fears, God opens the door for a blessing, and Royce Kavanaugh enters into her life, a firefighter built to rescue any damsel in distress. When a spark of attraction ignites, Candace and Royce soon discover there's more than one way to stop traffic.

In *A Baby for Christmas*, Book 2, yes, diamonds are a girl's best friend, but in Solae Wyatt-Palmer's case, she desires something more valuable. Captain Hershel Kavanaugh is a divorcee and the father of two adorable little boys. Solae has never been married and longs to be a mother. Although Hershel showers her with expensive gifts, his hesitation about proposing causes Solae to walk and never look back. As the holidays approach, Hershel must convince Solae that she has everything he could ever want for Christmas.

In *The Keepsake*, Book 3, Until death us do part…or until Desiree walks away. Desiree "Desi" Bishop is devastated when she finds evidence of her husband's affair. God knew she didn't get married only to one day have to stand before a judge and file for a divorce. But Desi wants out no matter how much her heart says to forgive Michael. That isn't easier said than done. She sees God's one acceptable reason for a divorce as the only opt-out clause in her marriage. Michael Bishop is a repenting man who loves his wife of three years. If only…he had paid attention to the red flags God sent to keep him from falling into the devil's snares. But Michael didn't and he had fallen. Although God had forgiven him instantly when he repented, Desi's forgiveness is moving at a snail's pace. In the end, after all the tears have been shed and forgiveness granted and received, the couple learns that some marriages are worth keeping

In *What God Has for Me*, Book 4, Halcyon Holland is leaving her live-in boyfriend, taking their daughter and the baby in her belly with her. She's tired of waiting for the ring, so she buys herself one. When her ex doesn't reconcile their relationship, Halcyon begins to second-guess whether or not she compromised her chance for a happily ever after. After all, what man in his right mind would want to deal with the community stigma of 'baby mama drama?' But Zachary Bishop has had his eye on Halcyon since the first time he saw her. Without a ring on her finger, Zachary prays that she will come to her senses and not only leave Scott, but come back to God. What one man doesn't cherish, Zach is ready to treasure. Not deterred by Halcyon's broken spirit, Zachary is on a mission to offer her a second chance at love that she can't refuse. And as far as her adorable children are concerned, Zachary's love is unconditional for a ready-made family. Halcyon will soon learn that her past circumstances won't hinder the Lord's blessings because what God has for her, is for her…and him…and the children.

In *Every Woman Needs a Praying Man*, Book 5, first impressions can make or break a business deal and they definitely could be a relationship buster, but an ill-timed panic attack draws two strangers together. Unlike firefighters who run into danger, instincts tell businessman Tyson Graham to head the other way as fast as he can when he meets a certain damsel in distress. Days later, the same woman struts through his door for a job interview. Monica Wyatt might possess the outward beauty and the brains on paper, but Tyson doesn't trust her to work for his firm, or maybe he doesn't trust his heart around her.

ANDERSEN BROTHERS SERIES

In *A Christian Christmas,* Book 1, Christian's Christmas will never be the same for Joy Knight if Christian Andersen has his way. Not to be confused with a secret Santa, Christian and his family are busier than Santa's elves making sure the Lord's blessings are distributed to those less fortunate by Christmas day. Joy is playing the hand that life dealt her, rearing four children in a home that is on the brink of foreclosure. She's not looking for a handout, but when Christian rescues her in the checkout line; her niece thinks Christian is an angel. Joy thinks he's just another man who will eventually leave, disappointing her and the children. Although Christian is a servant of the Lord, he is a flesh and blood man and all he wants for Christmas is Joy Knight. Can time spent with Christian turn Joy's attention from her financial woes to the real meaning of Christmas—and true love?

In *A Christian Easter,* how to celebrate Easter becomes a balancing act for Christian and Joy Andersen and their four children. Chocolate bunnies, colorful stuffed baskets, and flashy fashion shows are their competition. Despite the enticements, Christian refuses to succumb without a fight. And it becomes a tug of war when his recently adopted ten-year-old daughter, Bethani, wants to participate in her friend's Easter tradition. Christian hopes he has instilled

Proverbs 22:6, into the children's heart in the short time of being their dad.

In *A Christian Father's Day,* three fathers, one Father's Day and four children. Will the real dad, please stand up. It's never too late to be a father—or is it? Christian Andersen was looking forward to spending his first Father's Day with his adopted children---all four of them. But Father's day becomes more complicated than Christian or Joy ever imagined. Christian finds himself faced with living up to his name when things don't go his way to enjoy an idyllic once a year celebration. But he depends on God to guide him through the journey.

(All three of Christian's individual stories are in the Love for the Holidays anthology (Book 1 of the Andersen Brothers series)

In *A Woman After David's Heart,* Book 2, David Andersen doesn't have a problem indulging in Valentine's Day, per se, but not on a first date. Considering it was the love fest of the year, he didn't want a woman to get any ideas that a wedding ring was forthcoming before he got a chance to know her. So he has no choice but to wait until the whole Valentine's Day hoopla was over, then he would make his move on a sister in his church he can't take his eyes off of. For the past two years and counting, Valerie Hart hasn't been the recipient of a romantic Valentine's Day dinner invitation. To fill the void, Valerie keeps herself busy with God's business, hoping the Lord will send her perfect mate soon. Unfortunately, with no prospects in sight, it looks like that won't happen again this year. A Woman After David's Heart is a Valentine romance novella that can be enjoyed with or without a box of chocolates.

In *A Noelle for Nathan,* Book 3, is a story of kindness, selflessness, and falling in love during the Christmas season. Andersen Investors & Consultants, LLC, CFO Nathan Andersen (A Christian Christmas) isn't looking for attention when he buys a homeless man a meal, but grade school teacher Noelle Foster is watching his every move with admiration. His generosity makes him a man after her own heart. While donors give more to children and families in need around the holiday season, Noelle Foster believes in giving year-round after seeing many of her students struggle with hunger and finding a warm bed at night. At a second-chance meeting, sparks fly when Noelle and Nathan share a kindred spirit with their passion to help those less fortunate. Whether they're doing charity work or attending Christmas parties, the couple becomes inseparable. Although Noelle and Nathan exchange gifts, the biggest present is the one from Christ.

MAKING LOVE WORK SERIES

This series can be read in any order.

In *A Mother's Love,* to Jillian Carter, it's bad when her own daughter beats her to the altar. She became a teenage mother when she confused love for lust one summer. Despite the sins of her past, Jesus forgave her and blessed her to be the best Christian example for Shana. Jillian is not looking forward to becoming an empty-nester at thirty-nine. The old adage, she's not losing a daughter, but gaining a son-in-law is not comforting as she braces for a lonely life ahead. What she doesn't expect is for two men to vie for her affections: Shana's biological father who breezes back into their lives as a redeemed man and practicing Christian. Not only is Alex still good looking, but he's willing to right the wrong he's done in the past. Not if Dr. Dexter Harris has anything to say about it. The widower father of the groom has set his sights on Jillian and he's willing to pull out all the stops to woo her. Now the choice is hers. Who will be the next mother's love?

In *Love at Work,* how do two people go undercover to hide an office romance in a busy television newsroom? In plain sight, of course. Desiree King is an assignment editor at KDPX-TV in St. Louis, MO. She dispatches a team to wherever breaking news happens. Her focus is to stay ahead of the competition. Overall, she's easy-going, respectable, and compassionate. But when it comes to dating a fellow coworker, she refuses to cross that professional line. Award-winning investigative reporter Bryan Mitchell makes life challenging for Desiree with his thoughtful gestures, sweet notes, and support. He tries to convince Desiree that as Christians, they could show coworkers how to blend their personal and private lives without compromising their morals.

In *Words of Love,* call it old fashion, but Simone French was smitten with a love letter. Not a text, email, or Facebook post, but a love letter sent through snail mail. The prose wasn't the corny roses-are-red-and-violets-are-blue stuff. The first letter contained short accolades for a job well done. Soon after, the missives were filled with passionate words from a man who confessed the hidden secrets of his soul. He revealed his unspoken weaknesses, listed his uncompromising desires, and unapologetically noted his subtle strengths. Yes, Rice Taylor was ready to surrender to love. *Whew.* Closing her eyes, Simone inhaled the faint lingering smell of roses on the beige plain stationery. She had a testimony. If anyone would listen, she would proclaim that love was truly blind.

SINGLE TITLES

WWW.PATSIMMONS.NET

In *Talk to Me,* despite being deaf as a result of a fireworks explosion, CEO of a St. Louis non-profit company, Noel Richardson, expertly navigates the hearing world. What some view as a disability, Noel views as a challenge—his lack of hearing has never held him back. It also helps that he has great looks, numerous university degrees, and full bank accounts. But those assets don't define him as a man who longs for the right woman in his life. Deciding to visit a church service, Noel is blindsided by the most beautiful and graceful Deaf interpreter he's ever seen. Mackenzie Norton challenges him on every level through words and signing, but as their love grows, their faith is tested. When their church holds a yearly revival, they witness the healing power of God in others. Mackenzie has faith to believe that Noel can also get in on the blessing. Since faith comes by hearing, whose voice does Noel hear in his heart, Mackenzie or God's?

TESTIMONY: *If I Should Die Before I Wake.*

It is of the LORD's mercies that we are not consumed because His compassions fail not. They are new every morning, great is Thy faithfulness. Lamentations 3:22-23, God's mercies are sure; His promises are fulfilled, but a dawn of a new morning is God' grace. If you need a testimony about God's grace, then If I Should Die Before I Wake will encourage your soul. Nothing happens in our lives by chance. If you need a miracle, God's got that too. Trust Him. Has it been a while since you've had a testimony? Increase your prayer life, build your faith and walk in victory because, without a test, there is no testimony. (eBook only)

In *Her Dress*, sometimes a woman just wants to splurge on something new, especially when she's about to attend an event with movers and shakers. Find out what happens when Pepper Trudeau is all dressed up and goes to the ball, but another woman is modeling the same attire. At first, Pepper is embarrassed, then the night gets interesting when she meets Drake Logan. *Her Dress* is a romantic novella about the all too common occurrence—two women shopping at the same place. Maybe having the same taste isn't all bad. Sometimes a good dress is all you need to meet the man of your dreams. (eBook only)

In *Christmas Greetings*, Saige Carter loves everything about Christmas: the shopping, the food, the lights, and of course, Christmas wouldn't be complete without family and friends to share in the traditions they've created together. Plus, Saige is extra excited about her line of Christmas greeting cards hitting store shelves, but when she gets devastating news around the holidays, she wonders if she'll ever look at Christmas the same again. Daniel Washington is no Scrooge, but he'd rather skip the holidays altogether than spend them with his estranged family. After one too many arguments around the dinner table one year, Daniel had enough and walked away from the drama. As one year has turned into many, no one seems willing to take the first step toward reconciliation. When Daniel reads one of Saige's greeting cards, he's unsure if the words inside are enough to erase the pain and bring about forgiveness. Once God reveals to them His purpose for their lives, they will have a reason to rejoice.

In *Couple by Christmas*, holidays haven't been the same for Derek Washington since his divorce. He and his ex-wife, Robyn, go out the way to avoid each other. This Christmas may be different when he decides to gives his son, Tyler, the family he once had before the split.

Derek's going to need the Lord's intervention to soften his ex-wife's heart to agree. God's help doesn't come in the way he expected, but it's all good because everything falls in place for them to be a couple by Christmas.

In *Guilty of Love*, when do you know the most important decision of your life is the right one?

Reaping the seeds from what she's sown; Cheney Reynolds moves into a historic neighborhood in Ferguson, Missouri, and becomes reclusive. Her first neighbor, the incomparable Mrs. Beatrice Tilley Beacon aka Grandma BB, is an opinionated childless widow. Grandma BB is a self-proclaimed expert on topics Cheney isn't seeking advice—everything from landscaping to hip-hop dancing to romance. Then there is Parke Kokumuo Jamison VI, a direct descendant of a royal African tribe. He learned his family ancestry, African history, and lineage preservation before he could count. Unwittingly, they are drawn to each other, but it takes Christ to weave their lives into a spiritual bliss while He exonerates their past indiscretions.

In *Not Guilty*, one man, one woman, one God and one big problem. Malcolm Jamieson wasn't the man who got away, but the man God instructed Hallison Dinkins to set free. Instead of their explosive love affair leading them to the wedding altar, God diverted Hallison to the prayer altar during her first visit back to church in years.

Malcolm was convinced that his woman had lost her mind to break off their engagement. Didn't Hallison know that Malcolm, a tenth generation descendant of a royal African tribe, couldn't be replaced? Once Malcolm concedes that their relationship can't be salvaged, he issues Hallison his own edict, "If we're meant to be with each other, we'll find our way back. If not, that means that there's a love stronger than what we had." His words begin to haunt Hallison until she begins to regret their break up, and that's where their story begins. Someone has to retreat, and God never loses a battle.

In *Still Guilty*, Cheney Reynolds Jamieson made a choice years ago that is now shaping her future and the future of the men she loves. A botched abortion left her unable to carry a baby to term, and her husband, Parke K. Jamison VI, is expected to produce heirs. With a wife who cannot give him a child, Parke vows to find and get custody of his illegitimate son by any means necessary. Meanwhile, Cheney's twin brother, Rainey, struggles with his anger over his ex-girlfriend's actions that haunt him, and their father, Dr. Roland Reynolds, fights to keep an old secret in the past.

In *The Acquittal*, two worlds apart, but their hearts dance to the same African drum beat. On a professional level, Dr. Rainey Reynolds is a competent, highly sought-after orthodontist. Inwardly, he needs to be set free from the chaos of revelations that make him question if happiness is obtainable. To get away from the drama, Rainey is willing to leave the country under the guise of a mission trip with Dentist Without Borders. Will changing his surroundings really change him? If one woman can heal his wounds, then he will believe that there is really peace after the storm.

Ghanaian beauty Josephine Abena Yaa Amoah returns to Africa after completing her studies as an exchange student in St. Louis, Missouri. Although her heart bleeds for his peace, she knows she must step back and pray for Rainey's surrender to Christ in order for God to acquit him of his self-inflicted mental torture. In the Motherland of Ghana, Africa, Rainey visits the places of his ancestors but will he embrace the liberty that Christ's Blood really does set every man free.

In *Guilty by Association*, how important is a name? To the St. Louis Jamiesons who are tenth generation descendants of a royal African tribe—everything. To the Boston Jamiesons whose father never married their mother—there is no loyalty or legacy. Kidd Jamieson suffers from the "angry" male syndrome because of his father absentee but insisted his two sons carry his last name. It takes an old woman who mingles genealogy truths and Bible verses together for Kidd to realize his worth as a strong black man. He learns it's not his association with the name that identifies him, but the man he becomes that defines him.

In *The Guilt Trip*, Aaron "Ace" Jamieson is living a carefree life. He's good-looking, respectable when he's in the mood, but his weakness is women. If a woman tries to ambush him with a pregnancy, he takes off in the other direction. It's a lesson learned from his absentee father that responsibility is optional. Talise Rogers has a bright future ahead of her. She's pretty and has no problem catching a man's eye, which is exactly what she does with Ace. Trapping Ace Jamieson is the furthest thing from Taleigh's mind when she learns she is pregnant and Ace rejects her.

"I want nothing from you Ace, not even your name." And Talise meant it.

In *Free From Guilt*, it's salvation round-up time and Cameron Jamieson's name is on God's hit list. Although his brothers and cousins embraced God—thanks to the women in their lives—the two-degreed MIT graduate isn't going to let any woman take him down that path without a fight. He's satisfied with his career, social calendar, and good genes. But God uses a beautiful messenger, Gabrielle Dupree, to show him that he's in a spiritual deficit. Cameron learns the hard way that man's wisdom is like foolishness to God. For every philosophical argument he throws her way, Gabrielle exposes him to scriptures that make him question his worldly knowledge.

In *The Confession,* Sandra Nicholson had made good and bad choices throughout the years, but the best one was to give her life to Christ when her sons were small and to rear them up in the best Christian way she knew how. That was thirty something years ago and Sandra has evolved from a young single mother of two rambunctious boys, Kidd and Ace Jamieson, to a godly woman seasoned with wisdom. Despite the challenges and trials of rearing two strong-willed personalities, Sandra maintained her sanity through the grace of God, which kept gray strands at bay.

Now, Sandra Nicholson is on the threshold of happiness, but Kidd believes no man is good enough for his mother, especially if her love interest could be a man just like his absentee father.

THE CARMEN SISTERS SERIES

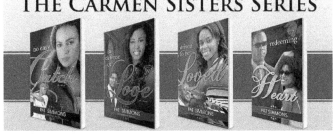

In *No Easy Catch*, Book 1, Shae Carmen hasn't lost her faith in God, only the men she's come across. Shae's recent heartbreak was discovering that her boyfriend was not only married but on the verge of reconciling with his estranged wife. Humiliated, Shae begins to second guess herself as why she didn't see the signs that he was nothing more than a devil's decoy masquerading as a devout Christian man. St. Louis Outfielder Rahn Maxwell finds himself a victim of an attempted carjacking. The Lord guides him out of harms' way by opening the gunman's eyes to Rahn's identity. The crook instead becomes an infatuated fan and asks for Rahn's autograph, and as a good will gesture, directs Rahn out of the ambush! When the news media gets wind of what happened with the baseball player, Shae's television station lands an exclusive interview. Shae and Rahn's chance meeting sets in motion a relationship where Rahn not only surrenders to Christ but pursues Shae with a purpose to prove that good men are still out there. After letting her guard down, Shae is faced with another scandal that rocks her world. This time the stakes are higher. Not only is her heart on the line, so is her professional credibility. She and Rahn are at odds about how to handle it and friction erupts between them. Will she strike out at love again? The Lord shows Rahn that nothing happens by chance, and everything is done for Him to get the glory.

In Defense of Love, Book 2, lately, nothing in Garrett Nash's life has made sense. When two people close to the U.S. Marshal wrong him deeply, Garrett expects God to remove them from his life. Instead, the Lord relocates Garrett to another city to start over, as if he were the offender instead of the victim.

Criminal attorney Shari Carmen is comfortable in her own skin—most of the time. Being a "dark and lovely" African-American sister has its challenges, especially when it comes to relationships. Although she's a fireball in the courtroom, she knows how to fade into the background and keep the proverbial spotlight off her personal life. But literal spotlights are a different matter altogether.

While playing tenor saxophone at an anniversary party, she grabs the attention of Garrett Nash. And as God draws them closer together, He makes another request of Garrett, one to which it will prove far more difficult to say "Yes, Lord."

In Redeeming Heart, Book 3, Landon Thomas (In Defense of Love) brings a new definition to the word "prodigal," as in prodigal son, brother or anything else imaginable. It's a good thing that God's love covers a multitude of sins, but He isn't letting Landon off easy. His journey from riches to rags proves to be humbling and a lesson well learned.

Real Estate Agent Octavia Winston is a woman on a mission, whether it's God's or hers professionally. One thing is for certain, she's not about to compromise when it comes to a Christian mate, so why did God send a homeless man to steal her heart?

Minister Rossi Tolliver (Crowning Glory) knows how to minister to God's lost sheep and through God's redemption, the game changes for Landon and Octavia.

In Driven to Be Loved, Book 4, on the surface, Brecee Carmen has nothing in common with Adrian Cole. She is a pediatrician certified in trauma care; he is a transportation problem solver for a luxury car dealership (a.k.a., a car salesman). Despite their slow but steady attraction to each other, neither one of them are sure that they're compatible. To complicate matters, Brecee is the sole unattached Carmen when it seems as though everyone else around her—family and friends—are finding love, except her.

Through a series of discoveries, Adrian and Brecee learn that things don't happen by coincidence. Generational forces are at work, keeping promises, protecting family members, and perhaps even drawing Adrian back to the church. For Brecee and Adrian, God has been hard at work, playing matchmaker all along the way for their paths cross at the right time and the right place.

**Check out my fellow Christian fiction authors writing about faith, family, and love. You won't be disappointed! www.blackchristianreads.com

Check out my Sweet Romance Reads authors at www.sweetromancereads.com

CPSIA information can be obtained
at www.ICGtesting.com
Printed in the USA
LVHW090211271018
595029LV00006B/118/P